DRAGONS

The Myths, Legends, & Lore

DOUG NILES, Dragonlance and Forgotten Realms series
author; Foreword by **MARGARET WEIS,** *New York Times*
bestselling novelist and co-creator of Dragonlance

Adams Media
New York London Toronto Sydney New Delhi

Adams Media
An Imprint of Simon & Schuster, Inc.
57 Littlefield Street
Avon, Massachusetts 02322

First Adams Media trade paperback edition APRIL 2017

ADAMS MEDIA and colophon are trademarks of Simon & Schuster, Inc.

For information about special discounts for bulk purchases, please contact Simon & Schuster Special Sales at 1-866-506-1949 or business@simonandschuster.com.
The Simon & Schuster Speakers Bureau can bring authors to your live event. For more information or to book an event contact the Simon & Schuster Speakers Bureau at 1-866-248-3049 or visit our website at www.simonspeakers.com.

Manufactured in the United States of America

6 2022

Library of Congress Cataloging-in-Publication Data has been applied for.

ISBN 978-1-4405-6215-0
ISBN 978-1-4405-6216-7 (ebook)

Interior illustrations from Marty Noble and Eric Gottesman, *Dragons and Wizards*, copyright © Dover Publications, Inc., 2003, ISBN: 978-0-486-99559-5; *Mythological and Fantastic Creatures*, copyright © 2002 by Dover Publications, Inc., ISBN: 978-0-486-99510-6; and Ernst and Johanna Lehner, *Big Book of Dragons, Monsters, and Other Mythical Creatures,* copyright © 1969 by Dover Publications, Inc., ISBN: 978-0-486-43512-1. Additional art © 123RF on pages 16, 18, 28, 58, 86, 112, 114, 151, 159, 168, 185, 202, and 211; © istockphoto on pages 51 and 154.

DEDICATION

To my colleagues and associates of the Alliterates Writing Society
(and I mean *all* of you—even the Bears fans):

Your friendship and counsel has meant so very much to me,
and I appreciate the solid advice and constructive criticism you've
shared with me over the past twenty years. Thank you!

CONTENTS

An Image for NIGHTMARES —And Dreams

 have been writing about dragons for about thirty years, starting with the first Dragonlance novel, *Dragons of Autumn Twilight*, published in 1984. I love having the opportunity to write about dragons, talk with them, gain their trust, work with them, even fly with them.

As you will learn in this book, dragons are universal. They exist in one form or another in almost every major culture in the world. Dragons have fascinated mankind for countless centuries and will continue to enthrall us, especially the artists and novelists, screenwriters, movie directors, animators, and special effects wizards who dream of dragons and work to bring those dreams to life.

For me, dragons are beautiful, magnificent, magical creatures in any world they inhabit. They are also the most intelligent, the most powerful, and the most dangerous. Humans are such puny creatures compared to dragons, which can slay us with the single swipe of a claw or the whoosh of their fiery breath. Yet we dare to be drawn to dragons, whether they are evil, greedy monsters who hide in caves and guard their treasure or whether they are friendly beings who permit us to fly on their backs.

Conversely, I like to think that dragons can be drawn to humans. They live for centuries and so they find human beings, with our short and frantic lives, fascinating. I like to write about dragons who have their own agendas. Often they use humans to achieve their own ends, but I also like to think that the dragons and humans can come to form a bond. Still, that bond is always tenuous.

No matter how close the relationship with humans, dragons remain aloof and mysterious. We are awed in their presence.

And always a little afraid.

—MARGARET WEIS

INTRODUCTION

"St. George he was for England,
And before he killed the dragon
He drank a pint of English ale
Out of an English flagon . . ."

—G. K. CHESTERTON,
"THE ENGLISHMAN"

Tales, images, myths, and legends about dragons form a part of the basic fabric of human storytelling. We have viewed dragons as gods and demons, as monsters, as misunderstood but sympathetic creatures, and as aspects of every imaginable variant of these many roles. Some dragons are scaly serpents, while others are covered with feathers or leathery skin. They can have wings or lack them—though almost all dragons can fly. Some dragons have human parts, most notably heads and torsos. Others mingle the paws, tails, beaks, and talons of birds, lions, tigers, monkeys, and the whole assortment of nature's menagerie.

Dragons are mysterious—part of their mystique lies in the fact that they are essentially aloof and unknowable to human minds. Dragons are magical, and many tales of dragonkind recall an ancient time when sorcery was believable, and the great, fanged serpents were tangible proof of magic. Often in story and myth, the fading of ancient magic is associated with the extinction of dragons.

Dragons—and dragon stories—are adaptable. One great example comes from the early Christian era: A warrior from Asia Minor—St. George—is said to have saved a princess from a dragon and by his action converted the population of a whole city in Libya to Christianity. Yet the nationality of the hero is often altered to match the setting of a different Christian nation. G. K. Chesterton's whimsical poem "The Englishman" imagines St. George as a proper, ale-drinking Anglo-Saxon!

The purpose of this book is to bring these tales together. Through it, we can unite in our imagination the scaly serpents of Norse myth with the wise and huge draconic powers of East Asia. With it, we can place the myths of the hybrid snake–human gods and demigods—the nāgas—of South Asia alongside the lethal wyrms of Greek mythology and the massively powerful Feathered Serpent hailed in virtually all of the early Mesoamerican civilizations.

But dragons are more than creatures of myth. We know dragons from literature, such as Smaug, presented by J. R. R. Tolkien in his epic fantasy *The Hobbit*. The genetically modified flying serpents of Anne McCaffrey's Pern science fiction series are creatures originating not from magic, but created by humans. Dragons appear in movies and are increasingly detailed as the quality of modern special effects continues to improve. Dragons feature prominently in adventure games and are, perhaps, the ultimate adversaries and omnipotent allies in both tabletop and video role-playing games. It is no accident that the original fantasy role-playing game is called *Dungeons & Dragons*!

Whether you view dragons as interesting creatures of fiction or as arcane images of ancient myth, you should find some intriguing tidbits and useful details in the pages of this book. Remember, keep your sword sharp and your lance at the ready. And hope your horse is as brave as you are . . .

Child   Are all the dragons fled?
Are all the goblins dead?
Am I quite safe in bed?

Nurse   Thou art quite safe in bed.
Dragons and goblins are all dead.

Child   When Michael's angels fought
The dragon, was it caught?
Did it jump and roar?
(Oh Nurse, don't shut the door.)
And did it try to bite?
(Nurse, don't blow out the light.)

Nurse   Hush, thou knowest what I said,
Saints and dragons are all dead.

Father (to himself)   O Child, Nurse lies to thee,
For dragons thou shalt see.
Please God that on that day
Thou may'st a dragon slay;
And if thou does not faint,
God shall not want a Saint.

—H. D. C. PEPLER, "DRAGON POEM," 1916

PART I

A UNIVERSAL SYMBOL

CHAPTER 1

ORIGINS
and Inspirations

he idea of the dragon is rooted in a deep and universal human apprehension about our own nature and the threats presented by the universe in which we live. Virtually every culture's mythology and bestiary includes some version of a mighty creature that in power, ability, and often wisdom and memory surpasses the limits of mere human capabilities. As our species came to dominate the rest of the natural environment, we confronted and eventually vanquished many creatures and forces that possessed the power to terrify and destroy us. Many of these potential foes are embodied in the myth of the dragon.

Forces of Inanimate Nature

Since primordial times, the brute forces of nature have presented a threat, generally inexplicable, to humankind. In an attempt to personify these threats, many of the traits of nature have been incorporated into draconic form, which may have made them more understandable—though certainly no less terrifying—to our ancestors.

Fire is a characteristic of many of the most lethal dragons of myth and lore, though by no means of all of them. Still, breathing fire is an unnatural ability, and when we think of a dragon's fiery breath, such thoughts tap into some of our deepest, most primeval fears. Exposure to fire in nature, whether as the product of volcanic eruption or the conflagration of a forest, presented humans in the past with a deadly threat that was easily attributed to malicious and serpentine foes.

Closely related to fire, the occurrence of *lightning*, whether as searing bolts lashing the ground or distant, flashing brightness flickering in the heavens, certainly suggested powers beyond imagining to early man. It was easy for people to invent powerful, magical beasts and attribute to them these mysterious explosions.

As with lightning and fire, massively powerful and unusual bursts of powerful *winds* were often thought to be the work of massive mythical beasts. Whether a dragon created a wind by flapping its broad wings or exhaling its powerful breath, it represented a possible explanation for a source of natural power that was clearly beyond the understanding of prehistoric humanity.

Water is not a force that we often attribute to a draconic source today, but in many of the earliest legends of dragon lore these serpents were beings that brought forth water. Some of these tales view the giving of water as a benign—even life-giving—gift. Some of these tales represent dragons as creatures that are friendly and helpful to humankind. Yet even the legends of ancient China, which often take a less antagonistic view of dragons than do the stories of the Fertile Crescent and Europe, portray hugely destructive floods as the work of dragons.

Inspirations from the Bestiary of Predators

Not surprisingly, the mythology of dragons incorporates some of the most lethal traits of the multitude of predators that has hunted, killed, and devoured humankind throughout the millennia. Storytellers regularly invoke many of these traits to describe the terrible power of the almighty dragon.

Snakes

The snake is probably the animal most commonly linked to the mighty dragons of myth. The dragon's body is typically described as serpentine, with a scaly skin and an ability to undulate and coil that is notably snakelike. Snakes have been a source of terror to humans throughout our existence, and even today many people are frightened of them to an irrational degree. Snakes lay eggs, and often live in underground lairs, suggesting further connection to draconic traits.

Furthermore, some snakes are venomous, and their poisonous bites— as well as poisoned blood or flesh—have been frequently described as being traits of ancient dragons. Other snakes can grow to tremendous size, and these massive constrictors, too, have been recognized as threats to humans.

In fact, there are good reasons for mankind's longstanding dread of snakes, and it is only natural that this dread has been twisted into a fundamental part of the draconic myth and legend throughout the ages.

Lizards

Closely related to snakes, the lizards of the natural world have contributed a certain array of their own traits to our understanding of dragons. Most dragons are assumed to have legs and powerful, taloned feet—an image clearly sourced more from lizards than snakes. Some Asian dragons have many pairs of legs and feet, like centipedes. By contrast, the Northern European image of the wyvern is essentially a two-legged dragon. Some lizards, most notably crocodiles, have been a predator of humans throughout the ages, and remain so to a limited extent even today. In Egypt, where Nile crocodiles were common and widely feared, the crocodile formed a basis for many interpretations of the wide pantheon of Egyptian gods.

THE KOMODO DRAGON

This large lizard is native to Indonesia and occasionally grows to more than ten feet long and weighs up to 150 pounds—certainly long enough to inspire dragon stories. Its teeth are up to an inch in length, and its body is covered by a protective armor of reddish-brown scales. Komodo dragons are fierce predators that charge their prey and attempt to rip out its throat.

Marine Predators

Many dragon myths refer to beasts that dwell, or can survive, in the water. These beasts are clearly inspired by dangerous fish such as sharks, barracudas, and eels, as well as marine mammals such as whales. Certainly, sharks have long been perceived as a frightening and dangerous threat, while the sheer size of whales naturally suggests beasts of a monstrous scale.

Birds

While even the largest birds do not generally present a physical threat to adult humans, these aviary creatures have long been esteemed for their almost mystical power of flight. Throughout the ages humans have watched birds in the air. No doubt our land-bound ancestors wished that they could emulate that liberating ability. Too, the physical weapon of a hawk, eagle, or condor—powerful talons, rending beak, as well as an ability to utter a piercing shriek, audible for miles—certainly helped to give inspiration to those mythmakers and storytellers who were inventing the earliest tales of mighty draconic beings.

"Fairy tales do not give a child his first idea of bogey. What fairy tales give the child is his first clear idea of the possible defeat of bogey. The baby has known the dragon intimately ever since he had an imagination. What the fairy tale provides for him is a St. George to kill the dragon."

—G. K. CHESTERTON, *TREMENDOUS TRIFLES*, ESSAY XVII, "THE RED ANGEL"

DIVERGENT
Tracks

ragons are beings of immense power, often unimaginably old, and are typically viewed as more akin to gods than to any mortal human or animal. It is this very awe-inspiring power that compels us to fear or revere them. The unlimited lengths to which that power can extend have caused people all over the world to imagine these beings as fantastic creatures dwelling well beyond the plane of normal existence.

Immortal Forces

Many of the oldest dragon myths view these great serpents as beings that existed in the time before man—in effect, as gods. This concept is in keeping with dragons as beings so incredibly magnificent and powerful that they are truly beyond the capability of mortal man to comprehend.

– 19 –

Dragons as Creators of the World

The myths of Babylon and Sumeria, of Egypt, India, Mesoamerica, and other places all offer examples of dragons as founding gods of the world. Tiamat, the great dragon of Babylon, is essential to that society's origin myth; while the Indian nāga, Shesha, does nothing less than support the world on his powerful, cobra-like hood.

"And Babylon shall become heaps,
a dwelling place for dragons, an astonishment,
and a hissing, without an inhabitant."

—JEREMIAH 51:37

Creators of Mankind

Many cultures have legends of serpents playing an instrumental role in the creation of human beings. In Mesoamerican myth, the Plumed Serpent (also called Feathered Serpent), Quetzalcoatl, journeys to the underworld to bring back, from previous eras of existence, components of life.

He then wounds himself and uses his own blood to transform those bits into humans. Many other peoples claim that they are direct descendants of serpents. The nāgas of South Asia are credited as being ancestors to entire nations, while the people of Japan believe that their emperors are the progeny of great dragons.

Dragons as Neutral Masters of Nature

Gods as diverse as Draco, in Greek mythology, and Zu (of Sumeria) are said to have possessed great power, capable of controlling wind, rain, and storm. The Japanese long worshipped Ryujin, a dragon said to be master of the sea, while the nāgas of South Asia are still viewed as very potent beings with huge power over water. The story of the nāga Apalala is one example of a cautionary tale in which a potent dragon is neglected by his human followers, much to their regret.

Bane of Humankind

Dragons are the adversaries of humankind in many myths and legends from cultures around the world. Because of their size, power, and special abilities, dragons make formidable foes, and these same traits make them worthy adversaries for humans who aim to achieve greatness.

The dragons of Greek myth, such as the Hydra that guards a magical spring or the golden serpent that protects the Golden Fleece sought by Jason, are typical of these adversarial symbols. The heroes who fight them usually need some sort of help from gods or magic; in Heracles's case, the hero is actually half-god himself.

Norse mythology, and the ubiquitous tales of fire-breathing dragons in Europe, also embody this type of dragon myth. The eight-headed dragon Orochi, of Japanese legend, is a classic example of the type of dragon that is a menace to the human race.

"It is possible that mankind is on the threshold of a golden age; but if so, it will be necessary first to slay the dragon that guards the door, and this dragon is religion."

—BERTRAND RUSSELL

GUARDIAN AND HELPER
OF HUMANKIND

The dragon that helps humans is more common in Eastern myth than in the stories of the West. South Asian nāgas and Chinese dragons all offer numerous examples of dragons that actively look out for people: helping, teaching, and protecting. One Chinese dragon, for example, is credited with giving the gift of written language to humans. In Mesoamerica, Quetzalcoatl is often hailed as a dragon who looks out for humans—which is a good thing, since so many other gods of that mythos seem eager to drink human blood whenever possible.

Dragons as Symbols

Dragons are used as symbols of many things. In Japan and China they symbolize the inherited status of an emperor's rule. In Christian myths, such as the tale of St. George and the dragon, the wyrm clearly symbolizes Satan. In many tales, dragons and other mythic serpents symbolize obstacles and challenges that seem insurmountable to mortal man. By defeating the dragon, the hero is showing that even the toughest adversary can, with the right combination of planning, equipment, and luck, be vanquished.

WORMS AND WYRMS

The word "dragon" comes from the Latin *draco*, a word the Romans got from the Greeks. In German, though, the word is *worm*, which in Old English became *wyrm*, a term many writers today use when referring to dragons. In several of his stories, the American horror writer H. P. Lovecraft refers to a mysterious volume *De Mysteriis Vermis* or *The Mysteries of the Worm* by Ludwig von Prinn. The title might, presumably, also be translated *The Mysteries of the Dragon*.

Guardian of Unimaginable Treasure

Many of the Indian nāgas, and a whole class of Chinese dragons—the Fut's-lung—are dedicated to protecting treasures within the earth from improper theft or exploitation. Fafnir, a dwarf of Norse legend, actually *becomes* a dragon because he has stolen treasures of great value and desires only to covet those treasures and keep them as his own. (Something similar happens to the character Eustace Scrubb in C. S. Lewis's Narnian novel *The Voyage of the Dawn Treader*.) Most of the dragons of European myth are credited with guarding hoards of valuables, and the attaining of those valuables can become the goal of a quest. The fire dragon that Beowulf fights at the end of the great king's life is so attuned to its vast hoard of treasure that it awakens from slumber and goes on a violent rampage merely because *one* precious object was removed by an interloping human. Similarly, Smaug in J. R. R. Tolkien's *The Hobbit* attempts to slaughter a party of dwarves when Bilbo Baggins, the titular hobbit, steals a cup from his hoard.

Symbols of Unattainable Goals

The Ouroboros is a serpent symbol known to almost every society in the world and is represented by a ring that shows a serpent biting its own tail. This symbolizes the implacable and inevitable nature of time, and seems to suggest that whatever we do, life will go on.

In China the dragon is one sign of the Zodiac, while the pearls of Chinese dragons are rare and mystical, and only very rarely can be held or possessed by a human. In Greek tales, the dragons guard treasures that are unique and godlike, crafted by immortal hands. It is significant that in those tales no mortal man could attack the dragon's treasure without significant, and usually god-based, intervention.

Finally, many dragon stories of European myth and folklore include a middle part of the story where heroic knights ride, one after the other, to do battle with the great serpent. But, alas, "none of them were ever heard from again."

THE OUROBOROS

An image of the Ouroboros appears on the cover of E. R. Eddison's 1922 fantasy novel *The Worm Ouroboros*. Nearly 3,500 years earlier, the image made its first appearance as part of the Egyptian *Book of the Netherworld*. In the Middle Ages, it was depicted on playing cards, including tarot decks. The symbol also was used in alchemy, the "science" of turning base metals into gold; as well, it was important in Gnostic religious beliefs.

"Why didst thou leave the trodden paths of men

Too soon, and with weak hands though mighty heart

Dare the unpastur'd dragon in his den?

Defenceless as thou wert, oh, where was then

Wisdom the mirror'd shield

Or scorn the spear?"

—PERCY BYSSHE SHELLEY (1792–1822),
"DESIRES AND ADORATIONS, XXVII"

PART II

CULTURAL
MYTHOLOGY

ALTHOUGH DRAGONS in some form or another are featured in the mythology and storytelling of virtually all human societies, the actual forms of the dragons, as well as their relationships with humankind, vary tremendously from place to place and throughout time. These next chapters will explore specific dragons as described by the peoples of many different cultures.

CHAPTER 3

DRAGONS
of Antiquity

s the earliest human societies began to develop the ability to produce food by domesticating animals and growing crops, they also began, of necessity, to live in towns and cities because they were more or less compelled to remain in one place to protect their means of food production. As a consequence of this increasing concentration of population, other traits of civilization appeared, including government, metallurgy, and other manifestations of technology . . . and writing.

Although storytelling has almost certainly been an aspect of human life since our ancestors had been nomadic hunter-gatherers clustered around campfires, the introduction of the written word allowed some of these stories to be preserved and retold throughout the years. Not surprisingly, some of the first dragon myths come down to us from some of the first societies that developed the art of writing.

Written language was first recorded in the Fertile Crescent of the Middle East, in the realms of Sumeria and Babylon (roughly, present-day Iraq). It spread through much of Asia, including India and China. It flourished in Persia, ancient Egypt, in the Semitic peoples of Palestine, and in other early civilizations of the Mediterranean, most notably the Greeks.

Dragons of Babylon, Sumeria, and the Fertile Crescent

Some of the earliest writings in human history dealt with the beings who had created and were presumed to still rule over the cosmos and the world. Naturally, some of these beings were dragons.

Making the World

Tiamat is the name given to the World (or Cosmic) Dragon in the early myths of both Sumer and Babylon. Tiamat and her consort, Apsu, existed together long before the creation of the world and humankind. Tiamat was a female who embodied the power of salt water and chaos, while Apsu was the spirit of fresh water and the all-encompassing void that was the nothingness of existence. Tiamat's body was huge and serpentine, including a long, coiling trunk and a skin impervious to weapons. She had a great head capped by two massive horns, with a long tail lashing from her hindquarters.

Tiamat and Apsu, according to the myth, created first the heavens and the world. These two progenitors contained the seeds of life for all living things, and after they made the world they created offspring who became the first gods of the world. Among these gods were Marduk, the fiercest and most powerful deity, and Ea, who had the uncanny ability to discern the future. Tiamat and Apsu also created the Girtablili, monstrous beings with the torsos and heads of humans set upon lower bodies of grotesque and powerful scorpions.

THE TALE OF TIAMAT

The story of Tiamat and Apsu is told in the Babylonian creation epic the *Enûma Eliš*, which survives from the ruins of the Library of Ashurbanipal in the ancient city of Niniveh. The story is written in Old Babylonian on clay tablets and was created some 4,000 years ago. This is one of the many examples of the dragon being used as part of a creation myth to explain the origins of the world and mankind. Interestingly, some scholars have suggested a connection between the dragon's name and the Greek word *thalassa*, or sea. The word may also have Semitic roots: *tehom*, meaning the deeps.

Fearing Ea's power more than that of any of the other gods, Apsu decided that this most wise of his offspring must be destroyed. Of course, since Ea knew the future, he perceived the threat to his life and he acted. He was able to tie Apsu with bonds and, when his father was immobilized, kill him. When the dragon goddess Tiamat learned of the death of her first, and only, consort she flew into a terrible rage and vowed that she would destroy Ea.

Once again Ea's mighty power gave him warning, for he saw that if the future led to a battle between Tiamat and him, he would inevitably be destroyed. While Tiamat took as her second consort another god, Kingu, Ea gathered all of the other gods together. As a group, they begged Marduk, the most powerful of their number, to do battle with the vengeful dragon. He agreed—but only on the condition that, if he was victorious, Marduk would be hailed by all as the supreme lord of all creation.

The two mighty beings, Tiamat and Marduk, girded themselves for battle. Marduk armed himself with a net, a club, and a bow that could shoot bolts of lightning. He mounted himself upon a chariot pulled by the four winds. Tiamat gathered her Girtablili scorpion-men and created many more fierce, bejeweled dragons to fight at her side.

The fight began with a cataclysmic clash of supernatural forces. Marduk used his net to ensnare Tiamat's monstrous allies, trapping and chaining them all. The great dragon lunged in to devour the warrior god, but when Tiamat's jaws spread wide Marduk launched one of his winds into her, holding her maw open so that he could fire his lightning bolts straight down her gullet and into her heart. One after the other, he blasted these lethal missiles into the goddess's flesh.

Tiamat's great heart finally ruptured, and after her death Marduk slashed her body into pieces. One part he cast into the heavens, where it still sparkles as the Milky Way. From the rest he formed the firmament that forms the landscape humankind first came to know. From the great dragon's blood, the rivers of the world were formed—including the Euphrates, which served as the source of so much of early civilization. Human beings themselves, so it was told, were formed from the pieces of Tiamat's monsters, those that had been caught in Marduk's net and, after the battle, slain and dismembered.

Zu and Enlil

In Sumerian myth, Enlil was the chief sky-god. His name is loosely translated as "lord of the storm" and he, with his wife Ninlil, presided over the vast pantheon of that ancient religion. Enlil presided over breath and wind, as well as all of the space in the cosmos. In much the same form, he was known as Bel to the Akkadians, and the Babylonian god Marduk also took on many of his attributes. His gentle breath was said to bring fertility to the land, and in the creation myth he was credited with dividing the sky from the world so that plants would have a place to grow. He had many lesser gods serving him, and one of these was Zu.

Zu represented an early concept of the dragon, as a descendent of birds. He could breathe fire and water and was pictured as a massive bird with the hands of a powerful man. In some images he is carved with the head of a lion and body of an eagle. A mingling of the pure waters of the sky and the solidity of the earth itself combined to give Zu life, and in his fearsome form he was commanded by Enlil to serve as a guardian of the palace and the sky-god's throne. It was said that even the other gods feared mighty Zu, who was regarded by many as a demon.

The role of servant and guardian did not suit the powerful being, however. In his greed and desire, Zu stole the Tablets of Destiny from his master. These scrolls supposedly allowed the bearer to determine the fate of all things, and Zu wanted this power for himself. He flew away from the palace of Enlil and hid them on top of a lofty mountain.

THE TABLETS OF DESTINY

These tablets appear in a number of places in Mesopotamian mythology. Made of clay and covered with cuneiform writing, they conferred divine authority upon Enlil. They are mentioned in the Sumerian poem *Ninurta and the Turtle* and in the Akkadian Anzû poem, as well as in other texts.

Zu knew that the other gods would be enraged by this theft and that they would try to retrieve the precious tablets. But the demon-bird had powers of his own: He was the master of storms and the bringer of the southern winds and thunderstorms. With these forces as allies, he remained on his lofty peak and relied upon the forces of gale, rain, thunder, and lightning to hold his pursuers at bay.

In all three of the cultural myths, Zu was eventually slain by the gods who pursued him and then attacked him in his mountain fastness. In the Babylonian tale, it was no less a personage than Marduk who slew the demon god, while in other myths Zu meets his fate through the attack of thunderbolts or through the magical arrows fired by a rival known as Ninurta, the sun god. In all of the stories, however, Zu craves and steals an irreplaceable treasure, and then guards the treasure in an inaccessible lair against the efforts of those who would retrieve them. Thus, in this legend from several millennia before the Christian era, we see many of the common threads of dragon tales throughout the ages.

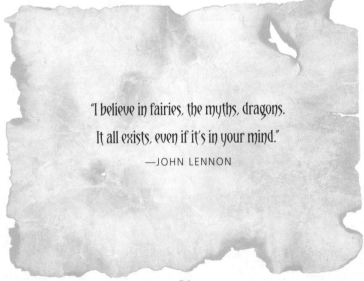

"I believe in fairies, the myths, dragons.
It all exists, even if it's in your mind."
—JOHN LENNON

Early Egyptian Dragon Myths

With abundant populations of both poisonous snakes and man-eating crocodiles, early Egyptians had many inspirations for dragon myths. Serpents, in particular, played roles as both evil and helpful deities, since they were said to watch over the dead. In consequence, images of serpents are often found on Egyptian tombs.

Apep

Apep was known as the mightiest enemy of Ra, the Egyptian sun god. Said to be a great snake, or serpent, and sometimes referred to as a dragon, Apep was greedy and covetous. Some descriptions claimed that Apep was as long as the height of eight men, and that his head was made out of flint. In other imaginings, he was miles long. He lived in the underworld, and believers imagined that he battled the sun every day, leading to nightfall and the hours of darkness.

Apep's roar was viewed as the cause of earthquakes and thunderstorms. Occasionally he became bold enough to attack Ra during the daylight, resulting in a solar eclipse. However, Ra's guardians were numerous and vigilant and always prevailed in a short time, bringing the sun back to its normal brightness. Eventually, as the civilization of ancient Egypt progressed, Apep's image and traits evolved to become Set, the god of evil in the Late Period of ancient Egypt.

THE EVOLUTION OF SET

Interestingly, in some earlier representations, Set is shown as a protector of Ra *against* Apep. There exist scenes depicting Set spearing Apep from the prow of Ra's night boat. In these scenes, Apep is sometimes shown as a serpent and sometimes as a turtle.

Nehebkau

This massive serpent served Ra. He guarded the entrance to the underworld, and thus aided the sun god in his daily battle with Apep. Some images of Nehebkau suggest that he was such a massive creature that the entire world rested upon him, with the serpent coiled so that his tail was held within his mouth. The serpent god was often portrayed as having the body of a snake, but the arms and legs of a human man.

Denwen

A serpent creature with a body made of fire, Denwen dates back to more than 2,000 years before the Christian era. He was so dangerous and imposing that he almost ignited a great fire that was set to consume all the gods of the pantheon. He was said to be thwarted by the pharaoh, thus justifying the monarch's right to rule.

Dragons of Greek Mythology

The modern word "dragon" traces its root to the Greek *drakon* and, as you'd expect, there are some notable examples of draconic myth in the early stories told by the Greeks. Generally, the dragons of Greek myth serve the roles as adversaries to heroic humans or demigods. Many people are familiar with the pantheon of Olympus in which Zeus and Hera, as the king and queen of the gods, preside over an unruly set of lesser gods. However, other gods, centered on the earth-mother Gaia, existed before the Olympian gods. The dragons of Greek myth are generally viewed as remnants of the rule of the elder gods.

Apollo and Drakon

One of the many offspring of the earth goddess Gaia is a huge serpent, usually with legs and clawed feet. He is known by the names Drakon, Draco, and Pytho or Python—all words that, obviously, have inspired modern terminology describing dragons and snakes. Drakon, like Gaia, predated the classic Greek gods.

Drakon was master of the Delphic oracle, the very center, or navel, of the world. That navel was represented at Delphi on the slopes of Mount Parnassus by a large rock called the Omphalos. The serpent god, it was said, entwined himself about this rock and protected it in his mother's name. For ages Drakon remained an immortal guardian of a most sacred site.

However, with the rise of Zeus and the Olympian gods of classic myth, Drakon was to meet his undoing. Zeus, as was his way, impregnated the goddess Leto. As she was preparing to give birth to twins—the gods Artemis and Apollo—Zeus's wife Hera, ever jealous of her husband's many infidelities, assigned Drakon to leave Delphi and pursue Leto around the world. In this way, she hoped, the rival goddess would not be able to give birth under the light of the sun.

Still, the twins were born, and when mighty Apollo came of age, he determined to take vengeance against the serpent god that had caused his mother such distress. At this time Drakon had returned to Mount Parnassus, and this is where Apollo attacked him. Under the sun god's onslaught Drakon made his way back to the oracle of Gaia at Delphi. There he took refuge in the sacred precincts of his mother's holiest site.

Apollo was not deterred, however. He burst through the gap in the rocks guarding the oracle site and attacked the great serpent with a barrage of arrows. In sight of his mother's most sacred place, Drakon perished, and Apollo buried his corpse under the great rock of Omphalos, the navel stone of the world.

THE POLITICS OF GREEK MYTH

Many scholars believe that the contemporary history of Greece, as the Hellenistic civilization arose in place of older cultures, was revealed by the actions of the Greek gods and their conflicts with older deities, such as Gaia and Drakon. In this story, the fact that the oracle of Delphi was established on the site of Drakon's grave is often considered symbolic. The more modern version of the tale was believed to have stamped out the older pagan cults of the earth-goddess. The priestess who presided over the oracle was often called Pythia, in acknowledgment of the older faith that had been defeated there.

The Hydra

The Hydra, with its multiple reptilian heads swaying on long, serpentine necks, is a classic form of the dragon. It appears in tales rooted in one of the most famous Greek myths. The story concerns Heracles (sometimes called Hercules), who—after committing an atrocity—was assigned twelve labors, or tasks, by Eurystheus, the ruler of Greece. For one of these tasks, Eurystheus commanded Heracles to slay the Hydra.

The Hydra was the spawn of two beings, Typhon and Echidna, known as the Father and Mother of All Monsters. Typhon was the most deadly monster in Greek mythology, the largest and most fearsome of all creatures, and had a hundred dragon heads (though in some accounts these heads were on his fingers). His wife, for her part, was half nymph and half snake. The goddess Hera trained the Hydra to be a challenge to Heracles as he went about accomplishing his quests.

The Hydra dwelt in the marshes of Lerna, near the site of the city of Argos. He guarded a cave that led to a portal to the underworld and emerged from this cave at night to devour cattle and unwary humans. So deadly was the Hydra's poisonous presence that his very footsteps were reputed to be

lethal, and his breath was powerful enough to kill anyone who breathed it. The Hydra's blood, too, was toxic; and he could survive the loss of his heads by the expedient growing back of two heads to replace each one that had been destroyed. Only the Hydra's central head, guarded by all the rest, was mortal.

Heracles sought the monster, accompanied by his nephew Iolaus. The two were watched over protectively by the goddess Athena.

Covering his mouth and nose with a protective cloth to filter the venomous air, Heracles approached the mouth of the cave wherein dwelt the Hydra. He fired a succession of flaming arrows into the darkness until the infuriated beast emerged and attacked. Each of the heads lashed out, snapping jaws striking at the hero.

Heracles struck back with his own weapon, though the stories vary in their accounts of what it was. Sometimes it was a great club; in other versions it was a sword or a farmer's sickle. He lopped off a head and the beast recoiled, but another pair of heads sprang from the wound. Holding his breath, Heracles repeated his attacks, but with each strike more heads grew.

With no apparent chance of winning, Heracles withdrew to make a plan. His nephew, who was perhaps inspired by Athena, had an idea. Iolaus built a fire and raised a burning torch.

"I'll sear the wound after you cut off the head!" he pledged. The two Greeks advanced in tandem to resume the attack.

Heracles struck again, slicing a head from the Hydra, and Iolaus instantly cauterized the wound. The seared stump flailed, but no heads regrew. Again and again the men repeated the process, gradually whittling away at the snarling, slashing monster. When only the central, immortal head remained, Heracles approached wielding a golden sword—a gift from Athena.

He struck the last head from the Hydra, but this head wouldn't die—it snapped and roared even as it thrashed about on the ground. Taking care to avoid the deadly poisonous blood that had splashed all over, Heracles hoisted the still-living head and threw it into a deep hole, tossing many huge rocks in on top of it, finally burying it where it could do no more damage.

As a final act, Heracles dipped his arrows in the deadly blood of the slain monster. These lethal missiles would prove useful as he turned to the rest of the heroic labors that had been placed upon him.

HOW MANY HEADS HAS THE HYDRA?

The most common number assigned to the heads of the Hydra is nine, though other sources claim up to a hundred, or even a thousand. The original poetry of the Greek classics is not specific, but it defines the number as "more heads than the vase-painters could paint."

The Dragon Ladon

Ladon is another fabulous dragon from the stories of ancient Greece. Like the Hydra, he had multiple heads; also like the Hydra, Ladon was one of the challenges—the eleventh—assigned Hercules by the king. Some claim that Ladon, and the garden where he was placed as a guardian, were on the Canary Islands, off the coast of Africa in the Atlantic Ocean. Regardless of whether or not the ships of ancient Greece were actually able to travel that far, the story is another compelling example of the Greek hero's strength and ingenuity.

Ladon was the guardian, placed by the queen of the gods, Hera, in the Garden of Hesperides. The dragon's task was to guard a tree bearing golden apples, as well as to guard the walled garden within which that tree produced its treasured fruit. The dragon had many heads—some claim as many as 100—and each head had two eyes. None of the heads ever needed sleep, so Ladon made a very effective, and watchful, guardian. The creature's body was long and serpentine, coiling about himself, and he was strong enough to squeeze the life out of a man—or, indeed, many men at the same time. The tail was thick and muscular, capable of lashing hard enough to

break a man's spine. Each of the heads was capable of speech, a different voice for each one, and the mouths were lined with ridges of razor-sharp teeth.

The serpent maintained guardianship of the tree by coiling himself around the trunk, his ever-watchful eyes flashing this way and that. The jaws were ready at a moment's notice to tear to pieces anyone or anything bold and foolish enough to enter the garden and try to steal the golden apples.

Heracles made his way to the wall outside the garden. He could see the golden apples on the tree rising above the wall, and he sensed the many-headed dragon nearly filling the garden around the base of the tree. His tactic, while perhaps not very sporting, was brutally effective. Taking the arrows he had poisoned earlier with the blood of the Hydra, he shot them over the wall and into the flesh of Ladon. After several of the arrows struck home, the many-headed dragon was overcome by the venom and collapsed, very near death. With his opponent thus neutralized, Heracles entered the garden and took the apples. As Heracles left to continue toward the last of his labors, Ladon's tail was still twitching, but the dragon could do nothing to stop the hero who had stolen his treasures.

THE DRAGON'S COSMIC FATE

Ladon eventually perished from the lethal arrows, though not before Jason and his Argonauts sailed past and saw the tail, still twitching. After Ladon's death, the goddess Hera placed him in the sky as the constellation Draco. There it still snakes through the heavens, surrounding the North Star just as steadfastly as it once surrounded the tree of the golden apples.

The Golden Dragon of Thebes

This dragon was the offspring of Ares, the Greek god of war, and it guarded a sacred source of water called the Castalian Spring. In some tales it is considered to be Drakon himself, the son of Gaia; in others, it is descended from that prototypical serpent. It figures in the Greek tale of the hero Cadmus, a prince of Phoenicia. The sister of Cadmus, Europa, was a woman of surpassing beauty. She was captured and borne away by none other than Zeus himself. The king of Phoenicia ordered Cadmus to go and rescue Europa and told him not to return without her. In the course of his wanderings, Cadmus killed the dragon and also founded the great city of Thebes.

A Brother's Quest

Accompanied by a set of bold companions, Cadmus searched for his sister for a long time. He concluded that she had indeed been taken by Zeus and despaired at his chances of challenging and besting that most powerful of all the gods. When Cadmus came to Delphi, home of the famous oracle, he decided to consult Pythia's advice on how to proceed.

The oracle told him to forget about Europa—he would never see her again. Instead, he received a puzzling command: He was to find and follow a unique cow, an animal marked by a half moon upon its side. When the cow finally collapsed from exhaustion, Cadmus should build a town upon that spot.

The cow was waiting for Cadmus outside the temple of the oracle, and he followed it to the land of Boeotia, where it finally lay down. Intending to sacrifice the animal to Athena as a blessing for the city he was about to found, he directed his men to go to the nearby Castalian Spring and to return with buckets of fresh water for the ceremony. Cadmus himself lay down to rest while his companions sought the water.

Some time later, the prince awoke, alarmed that his companions had not returned. He went to seek them beside the spring, and to his horror discovered their bodies, torn and bloody. They had been slain by some powerful force, something more violent than Cadmus could imagine. He looked up and saw a massive dragon, covered with glittering golden scales, poised to strike.

The Golden Guardian

Three rows of razor-sharp teeth lined the dragon's mouth. The body shimmered like a surface of overlapping coins of pure gold, and coiled like a snake, undulating as it lashed forward with that horrible gaping maw. Smoke and flames erupted from its flared nostrils, but the young prince steeled himself for a fight. He bore a heavy spear, and he thrust it against the monster's skin, but the scaly hide was too tough for him to inflict a serious wound.

Desperately, Cadmus parried the lashing fangs. The dragon reared, mouth still gaping, and the prince stabbed his heavy spear into the open mouth, past the rows of gleaming teeth, until the weapon lodged deep within the monster's gut. Hissing and thrashing, the dragon twisted and struck, but Cadmus danced out of the way. Black blood burbled from between the monstrous jaws, but still the dragon didn't die—instead it lunged after the prince.

But it wasn't quite fast enough to catch the nimble hero. His spear remained lodged within the monster's belly, so Cadmus hoisted a large rock and stood waiting. When next the dragon struck, it again came up short, the broad, flat head flopping to the ground before the Phoenician's feet. Cadmus threw down the rock and crushed the monster's skull, finally killing it.

The Final Test

Hearing an immortal command from the goddess Athena, Cadmus quickly pulled the fangs from the dead dragon's mouth and threw them onto the ground. Immediately the teeth sprouted, growing into the forms of full-grown, armed soldiers. A whole rank of these warriors appeared, brandishing swords and spears, squinting against the daylight as they looked for an enemy to attack.

Sensing his own vulnerability, Cadmus threw rocks into the midst of the newly formed men. The blows confused the men, who turned and began to fight among themselves. One after another of the magical warriors perished under the blows of their comrades, until only five remained. It was then that Cadmus stepped in, demanding the fealty of the remaining men. They knelt and accepted him as their leader. Following the command of the oracle, Cadmus bade these men help him found a city, and thus the great realm of Thebes was formed.

"Speak politely to an enraged dragon."

—J. R. R. TOLKIEN

The Dragon and the Golden Fleece

The story of Jason and the Argonauts is one of the most famous heroic tales of Greek mythology. Jason's crew of comrades included Heracles, the twins Castor and Pollux, Theseus, Orpheus the musician, and others. Aboard the fine ship *Argo*, they sailed the waters around Greece and even ventured into the Black Sea. They had many adventures, but their primary quest was the search for the Golden Fleece. Jason believed that if he returned with this treasure, he would win the throne of a kingdom that was rightfully his but that had been seized by his wicked half-brother, Pelias.

After a series of harrowing adventures, Jason finally arrived in Colchis, the land where the Golden Fleece was held. But even here, his quest was not so easily resolved.

Not surprisingly, the King of Colchis, Aeëtes, demanded three tasks of Jason before he would give up the treasure. The king believed that any one of the tasks, which included plowing a field with fire-breathing oxen, vanquishing a company of warriors, and facing and defeating the dragon that guarded the artifact, would prevent the Greek hero from making off with the Golden Fleece. Because of the intervention of the gods, however, Aeëtes's daughter Medea, who was a powerful sorceress in her own right, fell in love with Jason.

With Medea's aid, Jason mastered the first two tasks and turned to the fleece itself. It was nailed to a sacred oak tree, but before he went to take it Medea warned him that it was guarded by a fire-breathing dragon. This immense serpent was known as the Colchian Dragon and was another offspring of Typhon and Echidna. The beast had three tongues, and according to legend it never slept, rested, or otherwise lowered its vigilance.

But Medea told Jason that she knew how he could vanquish the Colchian Dragon. She covered Jason with a magic ointment, and then she gave him a cluster of herbs to hold as he went forward. As he approached the fleece the dragon emerged from its cave, rearing high and breathing a cloud of fire toward the hero.

Jason gagged and fell back, nearly blinded by the searing blast—but to his amazement he realized that Medea's ointment protected his skin and he was not injured by the infernal heat. Again he advanced, and again the dragon breathed fire. This time Jason held up the cluster of leaves the princess had given him. They burst into flames and spewed forth a column of blue, perfumed smoke.

The dragon inhaled the smoke and immediately began to sway and stagger, until it fell with a great crash onto the ground. It lay unconscious, stunned by the magical herbs, and Jason was able to tear the fleece from its tree. He made off with the treasure, and Medea joined him aboard the *Argo* as he sailed for home—where, to be sure, many more adventures awaited him.

MEDEA

Medea, in the continuation of the myth, proved to be a thoroughly ruthless and obsessed woman. When her father pursued the Argonauts in an effort to recapture the fleece, she killed her younger brother, Absyrtus, and scattered his limbs over the ocean so that Aeëtes would have to stop and collect and bury them. Later, when Jason became involved with the king of Corinth's daughter, Medea poisoned her. She took her revenge on Jason by killing her two children by him.

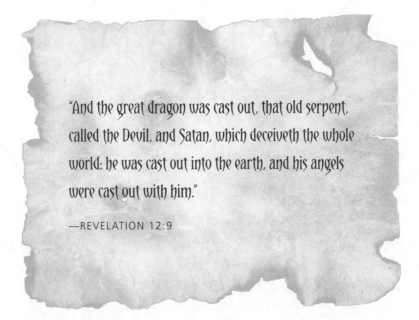

"And the great dragon was cast out, that old serpent, called the Devil, and Satan, which deceiveth the whole world: he was cast out into the earth, and his angels were cast out with him."

—REVELATION 12:9

Biblical Dragons

In both the Old and New Testaments, dragons are held up as mighty examples of evil. Often Satan himself is described as a dragon. The dragons of the Bible are not described as wyrms in the classic medieval sense, with wings, fiery breath, and so forth; but they are always depicted as some form of serpent or reptile (a crocodile is a common image). Variations include the terrible basilisk and the sea monster, or Leviathan.

Dragons of Hebrew Myth

The Book of Isaiah describes a Leviathan, or sea dragon, called Tannin—a word that, in modern Hebrew, means "crocodile." This dragon is compared to, and sometimes confused with, another sea monster called Rahab, mentioned in the Book of Psalms, which was supposed to dwell in the Red Sea. Some scholars feel that the story of Tannin was inspired by the earlier Sumerian/Babylonian myth of Tiamat. In any event, the name Tannin (as well as Rahab) was used to describe the land of Egypt after the exodus of the Israelites from the pharaoh's realm.

Job 41:21 speaks of a creature whose "breath kindleth coals, and a flame goeth out of his mouth," an image that clearly invokes the traditional picture of a dragon.

The Dragon of Revelation

The Book of Revelation, the last book of the New Testament, is probably the most apocalyptic section of the Christian Bible. It was written sometime during the last quarter of the first century of the Christian era, perhaps as early as A.D. 70, but most certainly before A.D. 100.

Among the most vivid images in Revelation is one describing a massive red dragon wreaking great destruction. The serpent's tail sweeps a huge number of stars out of the skies and sends them crashing to earth. The dragon then gathers allied angels and wages war against the Archangel Michael and his own supporters, in a clash that wracks all of heaven. Finally the dragon—"that old serpent, called the Devil, and Satan, which deceiveth the whole world"—together with the angels that fought at his side is expelled from heaven and sent to earth as punishment. Forever after, those celestial beings who have been rejected by the heavens are said to have been "cast out," and are characterized as "fallen."

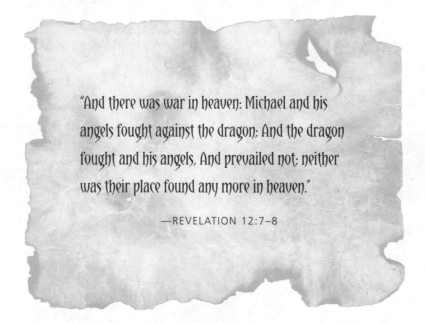

"And there was war in heaven: Michael and his angels fought against the dragon; And the dragon fought and his angels, And prevailed not; neither was their place found any more in heaven."

—REVELATION 12:7–8

Dragons of Early Christian Myth

Most of the Christian tales evoking dragons come not from the Bible but from the first centuries of the Christian era. These stories often tell of martyrs whose sacrifice in the name of the faith could be held up as an inspiration. Such tales aided the church in its ongoing effort to seek and gain converts.

The Dragon and St. George

While the dragon famously destroyed by St. George dwelt in Libya, the story formed a standard epic throughout the Christian societies of the world. It found a special niche in the age of chivalry, in northern Europe, most notably in France and England. The tale was first written down during the sixth century and is supposed to have occurred around A.D. 300. Early artistic depictions of it appear from the eleventh century on. It was commonly used to illustrate the power of the Christian faith over the forces of evil.

At the beginning of the fourth century, the Roman Empire was in its twilight but still sprawled across the Mediterranean region from Spain to Turkey, encompassing much of the Middle East, North Africa, and even Gaul (France) and England. Although Christianity had been a growing religion for three centuries, it was not yet officially approved by the empire; that would not happen until Emperor Constantine decreed tolerance for Christianity in 313. Before that time, Christians were subjected to persecution throughout the empire.

George, however, according to the legend, was undeterred and practiced the faith even though he was a soldier in the Imperial Guard. However, when Emperor Diocletian passed a law decreeing that all Christians should face the death penalty, George left the service of the empire and returned to his native land of Cappadocia, in what is now central Turkey. George donned armor and hoisted a shield, both emblazoned with the Christian cross. Girding his horse in gold, he took up his lance and began to roam the land and spread the Christian faith. His journeys took him along the southern coast of the Mediterranean Sea where, at last, he came to Libya, and to the city of Silene.

There, in a lake by the city, dwelt a venomous and deadly dragon, a creature that had come down from the inland mountains to prey on the herds of cattle and sheep maintained by the people of Silene. Finally the dragon killed and devoured a young shepherd, and the king was forced to negotiate terms with the monster.

The people of Silene placated the dragon for some time by offering it a pair of sacrificial sheep every morning. So long as the sheep were staked out beside the lake where the dragon dwelt, the monster would emerge, claim the sacrificial animals, and return to its watery lair, leaving the rest of the herds—and the people—alone.

Finally, so goes the legend, all the sheep of Silene had been given up. The king and his council came to an awful decision: The dragon would have to be placated with the children of the town. For some bleak time a child, chosen by lottery, was taken to the lakeshore and tied to a rock. The dragon came forth and ate the child, and thus left the craven people of Silene to their petty endeavors.

One day, as fate would have it, the lottery threw up the name of the king's own daughter as the child who should be the dragon's meal. The monarch despaired and offered all of his treasures, to be divided among his people, if only the princess would be spared. The people of Silene, discouraged and bitter because of the loss of so many of their own children, wanted nothing to do with the king's pleas. So it came to pass that the princess, dressed as a bride, was taken from the city and tied to the rock beside the lake, where she would have to spend a horrible night awaiting her grisly fate.

The Knight-Hero Arrives

It was then that George, mounted on his gold-bejeweled horse and bearing his lance, with his shield and armor emblazoned with the bold cross of Christendom, came upon the princess in her despair. He offered to save her, but the brave lass pleaded with him to continue past, warning him that the dragon would merely kill him as well as her. The knight, of course, refused her plea—and, before he had a chance to do anything else, the dragon reared out of the lake and attacked.

George made the sign of the cross, hoisted his lance, and charged the dragon at the water's edge. His weapon pierced the creature's scaly breast and it collapsed, thrashing and wounded but not mortally hurt. George commanded the princess to give him her "girdle"—probably what modern society would call her belt—which the brave knight wrapped around the dragon's neck. The beast was thus subdued.

George hoisted the princess onto his horse and, tugging on the end of the leash, pulled the captured dragon behind him as he rode up to the city of Silene. The people were terrified at the dragon's approach and at first wanted nothing to do with this mad warrior who had presumably brought doom upon them.

But George was not one to miss a chance at a mass conversion. He preached to the people that it was Christ himself who was their deliverer. If the king and his men would allow themselves to be baptized, George promised, he would slay the dragon in front of them, and their terrible crisis would be solved. Naturally, the people of Silene agreed. The king and the other men were baptized, and George slew the dragon by lopping off its head. According to the legend, it took four massive oxcarts to haul the dragon's remains away from the city.

The tale has various endings—in at least one of them, George marries the princess; but in others he continues his wandering and adventures and is eventually tortured and martyred in the Christian cause. Some centuries after his death, he was declared to be a saint in both the Eastern and Western branches of Christendom.

ST. GEORGE AND ISLAM

St. George is one of the few Christian saints to also be venerated in the Muslim world. He is sometimes identified with al-Khidr, a mysterious figure in the Koran who interacts with Moses. St. George is said by adherents of the Islamic faith to have killed a dragon near Beirut in Lebanon, where there existed, for many years, a shrine to him.

Margaret the Virgin

This saint is also known as Margaret of Antioch, and she lived during the very first centuries of the Christian era. Her father was a pagan priest, and when Margaret converted to Christianity he ordered her from his home, after which she lived in the countryside of what is now Turkey, tending sheep. She was a very beautiful woman, and when the Roman governor of the province spotted her he was taken with her beauty and asked her to marry him. When he required that she renounce her faith, however, she refused.

The governor ordered her thrown into his dungeon, where she was tortured relentlessly, but still she maintained her Christian beliefs. Finally, Satan himself decided he'd had enough of her stubbornness. He appeared as a dragon and set to gulping down and devouring the faithful virgin. However, her tormentor had neglected to remove the vestments of her faith, and the cross that she wore caused such distress to the dragon's gut that he had no choice but to vomit her forth.

This being a martyr's story, though, there is no happy fairy tale ending. Following her miraculous escape from the dragon, the governor ordered Margaret put to death, which is supposed to have occurred in the year 304. The young woman's faith and martyrdom, together with the dramatic dragon legend, became part of Christian legend. The story gained great prominence, particularly during the Crusades, when Christian knights spent extensive time in the Middle East and Turkey. Margaret is a saint in both the Roman and Orthodox churches and was one of the voices who spoke to Joan of Arc during the latter's travails. Today there are several hundred churches and chapels in England devoted to Margaret the Virgin.

Saint Patrick and the Snakes of Ireland

Saint Patrick is of course the most famous early Christian of Ireland and is said to have carried the word of the Gospel around the Emerald Isle during the first half of the fifth century. A great deal of myth surrounds his heritage and life, but it is generally believed that he was born in Britain to a Christian family. At the age of sixteen he was captured by Irish raiders and carried to that island, where he lived as a slave for some years. In his twenties, he escaped and returned to Britain. Later he returned to the island to embark upon his life's work, which resulted in the conversion of much of Ireland's population to Christianity.

One of the most enduring myths about Saint Patrick relates that as he was fasting for forty days on a mountain, and in the midst of his meditations, he was attacked by snakes. In his righteous fury, he called upon the force of the Lord, and drove all of the snakes across all the width and breadth of Ireland into the sea, where they drowned.

Modern science gives pretty solid evidence that Ireland never had any indigenous snakes, certainly not since the end of the last ice age. However, the druids who were the main religious competition to Christian monks were known to emblazon tattoos of snakes and other serpents on their limbs. This seems to be a classic example of the serpents being used as symbols of, if not the Devil, then at least the pagans whom the Christians felt duty-bound to overcome.

CHAPTER 4

DRAGONS
of East Asia

 ragons play a rich and significant role in the mythology of the great eastern civilizations. Three great cultural traditions, in China, Korea, and Japan, all express different variations on the roles of the great serpents. The Chinese myths are the oldest; and the first of them arose nearly at the same time the early civilizations of the Fertile Crescent began to take shape. One of the earliest images of a dragon, a brightly colored mosaic in seashells set into the ground, was found in a Chinese tomb dated to about 6,000 years ago.

Although the dragons of East Asian culture are powerful and capable of doing a great deal of damage, they are generally not regarded as the greedy, destructive, and wicked wyrms that are featured in European myths. Many tales of Asian dragons show the serpents helping humankind or even befriending specific men and women. Even when a dragon is unhelpful, a sympathetic explanation is usually presented for its behavior. Of course, there are exceptions—as described later in this chapter in the Japanese myth of the Yamata no Orochi.

Dragons of China

Chinese dragons are often referred to by the word *lung* (alternately, *long*, depending on the style of transcription used to translate Chinese characters). Though they varied tremendously in their individual traits and acts, certain aspects of the lung were said to be universal. All Chinese dragons are described as sharing nine features:

1. A head like that of a camel
2. A scaly body like a carp's
3. Horns upon its head like a stag or an antelope
4. Eyes like a rabbit's
5. Ears like a bull's
6. The neck of a snake
7. The belly of a clam
8. The paws of a tiger
9. The claws of an eagle

Chinese dragons can be petulant and proud, but are never described as purely evil. They are often associated with water, and many myths suggest that they dwell most comfortably in water, even though they can live on the land and fly through the air. Each of the seas along the coasts of China is credited with having a specific dragon that resides there.

Life Cycle of a Dragon

The life cycle of a Chinese dragon has been fairly well defined in litera-ture and folk tales. The female lung lays her eggs in shallow water, near the banks of rivers or the shores of lakes. These eggs are scattered along the beds of the waterways and look like marvelously beautiful stones. Each egg requires a thousand years of incubation before it is ready to hatch. When the magical moment of birth arrives, and the first crack appears in a dragon egg, each of the parents utters an eerie, unnatu-rally loud cry. It is said that the father's cry will cause the winds to swirl furiously, and that the mother's soothes the agitated breeze.

When the cracked egg actually breaks open, the infant dragon emerges to a chorus of crashing thunder and driving rain. These portents are only appropriate because throughout Chinese mythology dragons have long been hailed as having great power over water and weather. After hatching, the young dragons emerge from their watery birthplaces and require around fifteen centuries to attain full size and 500 more years to grow the horns that symbolize their complete maturity.

TAKING WING

Most Chinese dragons are not pictured or described as having wings. However, it has been said by legend that when a dragon reaches the age of 1,000 years, it can grow wings if it wants. These branchlike appendages emerge from its flanks but are not necessary for flight. Indeed, all Chinese dragons, whether or not they have wings, can fly.

Historical Significance of Chinese Dragons

Stories of dragons in China date back more than 7,000 years. One legend has it that Buddha called all the animals in the world to journey to him. As it turned out, only twelve of the animals could reach the Buddha, and these twelve became the signs of the Zodiac. One of them, of course, was the dragon.

Many Chinese believed that people were distant descendants of dragons, through the goddess Nu Kua, who was half mortal and half dragon. Her children could shift between dragon and human form with ease. They could also increase or decrease their size, fly through the skies—even as high as the heavens—and without breathing dive to the very depths of the seas.

RULE OF THE DRAGONS

Chinese emperors were long hailed as being the sons of dragons. This was commemorated by special robes, inscribed with the sign of the celestial dragon, which only emperors were allowed to wear. Yellow dragons with five claws on each foot are typical imperial symbols. These dragons could only be depicted on the robes and other garments worn by the emperor, or on the flags and other heraldry associated with his station. Imperial dragon symbols are found in such places as Beijing's Forbidden City, the former residence of the emperors of China.

Categories of Chinese Dragons

The dragons, or lung, of the Chinese mythos were universally powerful, long-lived, and wise beings. However, they differed widely from each other, and took several distinct forms.

Tien-lung

The Tien-lung were the celestial dragons, and held the highest places in the dragon hierarchy, guarding and dwelling in the palaces of the gods. The greatest of the Tien-lung was said to be the ruler over all dragonkind. These dragons are rare, and generally thought to be benign. One of the earliest mentions of a Tien-lung describes a man who was a skilled painter. He created many pictures of beautiful dragons on the walls of his house, and his work was so beautiful that it attracted the attention of one of the celestial dragons. That dragon came to see the pictures directly, but its presence was so awesome that the painter became frightened and ran away.

Shen-lung

The Shen-lung were the so-called spirit, or spiritual, dragons. Their primary function was to control the wind and the rain, and to bring storms upon the world. These dragons were described as having scales of azure and, because they were responsible for rain, were especially important to farmers. People would take great care to avoid offending a Shen-lung, since they knew that such an insult could result in a terrible flood or a drought. This dragon was so huge that when he floated in the sky he stretched from horizon to horizon, and no person could get a glimpse of the monstrous creature in his entirety.

Legends say that the Shen-lung, because of his great power, was prone to laziness. In order to avoid the tasks associated with his vast duties, he would shrink to the size of a mouse and then hide in a haystack, a nest of roots, or even a house. When lightning struck any of these places, it was said that the god of thunder had sent his servant to seek out the lazy Shen-lung.

Especially exalted Shen-lung are called Imperial Dragons and were distinguished because they had five toes.

Fut-lung

The Fut-lung (or "Fut's-lung" or "Fucanlong") were the dragons of the underworld. One of their primary functions was to serve as guardians of treasures, including metals and jewels that were mined from the earth. They also guarded manmade treasures that were buried for concealment. Volcanic eruptions were supposed to be caused by a Fut-lung dragon bursting out of the earth. Each of these dragons kept a valuable pearl as a talisman; these pearls play an important role in many Chinese tales of dragons.

Ti-lung

These dragons are called the earth dragons. Oddly enough, like the Shen-lung, they were actually masters of water, but instead of rain and weather they watched over rivers, lakes, and streams. It was said that the Ti-lung spent autumn in the heavens and spring in the sea.

OTHER CHINESE DRAGON TYPES

As many as five other classes of dragons are parts of Chinese mythology, though they are not as numerous or as significant as the four *lungs* previously described. These other classes include:

- Coiling Dragons, which live in the seas
- Horned Dragons, said to be among the mightiest of all dragons
- The Yellow Dragon, which is known for his learned bearing and is said to have given the gift of writing to humans
- The Winged Dragon, which by legend is credited with controlling the Yellow River, using its tail to dig long channels to divert the flowing water
- The Dragon Kings, who were the four dragons said to reside in, and control, the seas around China

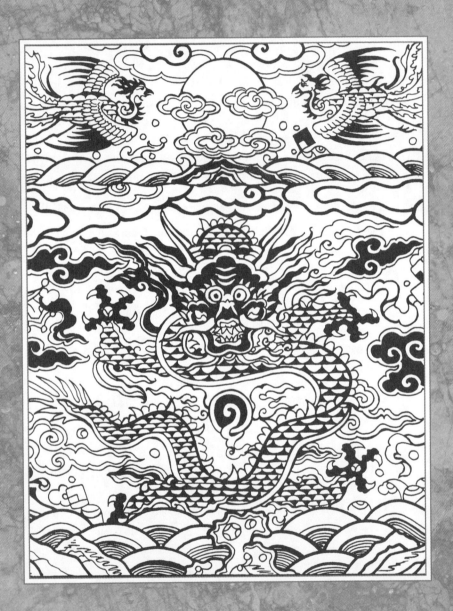

The Water Dragon of Beijing

Although the dragons of Chinese mythology are often portrayed as wise, benign, and helpful to mankind, that is not always the case. One story involves a jealous dragon who resented human intrusion and took dramatic action to make his displeasure known. The occasion was the initial establishment of what would become the thriving city of Beijing.

One legend of the founding of this great city comes from the beginning of the Ming Dynasty, around 1370. (Beijing's origins lie in the eleventh century B.C.) One of the ancestral Chinese gods, Nocha, is said to have advised the emperor as to where the city should be placed. At the time, the land where the capital now exists was a broad and stagnant lowland, wet with marshy swamp and brackish water.

The marsh was ruled by a clan of dragons who were quite happy there. They took a very dim view of operations when the emperor appointed a great builder, Liu Ji Bowen, to begin construction of a vast city in the dragons' marshland. As men spread through the countryside, digging ditches, laying down roads, and beginning to place the foundations for great buildings, the dragon who ruled the family decided that he would make the audacious humans regret their choice of location.

Like many Chinese dragons, this one was a highly magical creature who could change his shape at will. He made himself and his mate to appear as an old man and an old woman. They put two large water jars onto a cart and made their way to see the emperor. Bowing and showing the imperial leader all respect, they humbly asked permission to be allowed to leave the city with their water jars.

Thinking very little about the request, the emperor bade them to go. What he did not know was that the dragons had taken all of the fresh water from the region around Beijing and magically stored the liquid in the two jars. They left the city in the evening and made their way into the distant hills.

The next morning the city awakened to discover itself in the midst of a sudden and devastating drought—no water was to be found anywhere, in the wells or the swamps or the ponds that had previously dotted so much of the landscape. The emperor despaired, and his people panicked—all but the great builder, Liu Ji Bowen, who consulted the god Nocha and learned what had happened.

Acting quickly, Liu sent word to all the gate guards in the city to find out who had departed the city the previous night. He learned that the elderly couple, with their two large jars, had left the city heading toward the western hills. He knew that, if they reached those hills and spilled the water there, the city would be dry forever. So the builder asked for a member of the emperor's guards to volunteer to save the day.

One brave soldier, Gaoliang, offered to perform the task. The builder gave him a long spear and told him to hurry after the old man and old woman. When he found them, he was to break the jars quickly, one right after the other, then turn around and flee back to the city as fast as he could run. He was warned not to look behind him but to keep on running.

Carrying the spear at his side, the bold warrior jogged along the western road, traveling so fast that he caught up to the old couple—who plodded along very slowly indeed—by midday. There was no clue that these two were dragons; they looked like elderly Chinese peasants. Gaoliang approached as stealthily as he could and suddenly stabbed his spear into the nearest of the water jars.

The clay vessel shattered, but as the soldier drew back his arm to thrust at the second jar a deluge of water flooded from the broken jar, forcing him back. Before his horrified eyes he saw the old man swiftly change shape, coiling and growing, rising to loom before him as a mighty dragon.

There was no chance to break the other jar, so Gaoliang turned and sprinted back to the city as fast as he could run. He heard the surging and churning of a vast flood roaring behind him, and he dropped the spear and sprinted with every bit of speed he could muster. Soon he came within sight of the city, but at the very gate he had departed he saw a crowd of people gesturing and shouting at something that was behind, and pursuing, him. Gaoliang faltered in his flight, turning to look, and a massive curl of churning water swept over him, smashing him down and drowning him.

The waters surged up to the city but did not inundate it. The water from the jar that the soldier shattered was brackish and tainted, but it was enough to grow crops. Still, the legends claim that the best, purest water was taken away forever in the other jar, the one that Gaoliang did not have a chance to shatter. Even so, his heroism was recognized, and the river that formed at the western gate of the city was named for him. So too was a beautiful arched bridge that was erected over that river in 1764. The Gaoliang Bridge is a work of stunning artistry that still stands today.

Pearls of the Dragons

Many stories claim that Chinese dragons carry valuable pearls with them, often holding them beneath their chins. These pearls can be bestowed as gifts or stolen as treasures. They are central to several tales of the great lung dragons.

The Pearl of Hai Li Bu

A kindly man named Hai Li Bu was walking along the shore of a stream near his village one day when he heard a great squawking in the reeds. Pushing his way into the marsh he saw that the source of the noise was a large white goose. Wings flapping and beak snapping, the goose was striking at a small snake that was coiled against a rock on the shore. The man felt sympathy for the helpless snake, so he used his walking staff to drive the goose away.

When the angry bird was gone, the snake uncoiled and, to Hai Li Bu's astonishment, rose up to stand before him as a beautiful young woman. She said that she was the daughter of the Dragon King, and that the man who had saved her life deserved a great reward. She took from her pouch a small, shining pearl, and handed it to Hai Li Bu.

"Hold this stone and you will understand the speech of the animals," said the girl. "You may use this knowledge as you wish—but you cannot tell other humans what the animals are saying, or you will be turned to stone."

Hai Li Bu cherished his gift and for many years enjoyed listening to the words of the birds and the goats and the dogs that lived in and around his village. He minded his tongue for all those years, however, remembering the warning that accompanied his magical pearl.

One day, however, he heard the birds chattering in great excitement and fear about a terrible flood that was even then rushing down the river valley. The birds took flight, warning each other that the whole land—including the village—would be washed away by the terrible waters. Hai Li Bu was too kindly a man to keep this news to himself. Instead, he rushed about the village, warning his neighbors of the coming flood. They all ran to the hills, taking their children and their elders with them as they sought shelter on high ground. From their shelters, they looked back to see the flood rush through the village. In the middle of the foaming waters, and soon covered under the rushing tide, stood a stone statue—all that was left of Hai Li Bu.

The Grass-Seller's Pearl

A hardworking boy lived with his mother beside the Min River. They were very poor, but the boy was able to make a little money by slicing sheaves of fresh grass with his sickle, then carrying the bundles to his neighbors so that they could feed their pigs, sheep, and cows. Often he could find plenty of lush grass right near his village, but during drier times he had to wander very far afield to find enough green grass to cut and sell.

During one very dry summer, he journeyed farther up the river valley than he ever had before, and he discovered a patch of tall, bright green grass. For many days he walked to that place, cutting as much grass as he could carry, and then carrying his crop back to the village. No matter how much he cut, he always found the patch of grass to be full and lush when he returned the following day.

Still, because of the distance he wasn't able to bring back enough grass to make even the small amount of money he and his mother needed for food. He decided to see if he could replant some of his precious fodder, so he took along his spade and cut out a square of the grass with its roots and dirt intact. When he lifted it up he was surprised to see a large, bright pearl lying in the hole. He carried both the square of grass and the pearl back to his mother. She was delighted at the stone, and hid it in her rice jar, which had only a few grains of rice in it at the time.

In the meantime, the boy planted his square of grass near the almost-dry river beside their house. He ran outside the next day full of hope but was dismayed to see that the grass he had so laboriously transplanted had died, turning brown and withered overnight. His mother told him not to worry, however, since the pearl that he had found was worth enough to buy them a lot of food. She went to retrieve the stone, and they were both astonished to see that the rice jar was full to the top! Realizing that the pearl was magic, the next night they placed it in their money jar—which contained only a few paltry coins. When they awakened, the jar was full of shiny coins.

The two knew they would have to keep the existence of the pearl secret, but even so people in the small village couldn't help but notice that the small family had obviously come into some money. It wasn't very long before a pair of thieves broke into the house and began to ransack everything. The boy was terrified they would find his pearl, so he took up the money jar to give to the thieves—but he sneaked the pearl into his hand and swallowed it.

Immediately his gut was wracked with a terrible, fiery pain. The boy ran to the well and drank pitcher after pitcher of water, but the fire only seemed to burn hotter. He stumbled to the riverbank and lay down with his head in the water, still trying to drink. Before his mother's—and the thieves'—horrified eyes the boy's body began to grow huge. Scales broke out along his skin, and his head sprouted mighty horns. Very quickly he became a huge, coiling dragon. Immediately rain poured from the clouds, breaking the drought that had parched the land. But the huge dragon couldn't live on the shore—and with one anguished glance back at his mother, the boy-become-dragon plunged into the river and swam away.

DRAGONS AND TREASURE

No one quite knows why dragons are associated with precious things such as gold, silver, and gems. The tradition seems to extend around the world, from the dragon hoards of Western European wyrms to the precious pearls of Eastern dragons. Eastern dragons, however, as some legends portray, place more value on wisdom than treasure. This may be why Eastern dragons are generally more benevolent than their Western counterparts.

Tchang's Pearl

A magic dragon's pearl is prominently featured in another story about a poor boy, Tchang, who lived with his mother at the shore of a large but fishless lake. The tale presents a strong moral that selfless behavior can eventually be rewarded.

Tchang wanted an explanation from the gods of the sad state of his life. To this end he embarked upon a quest to confront the divine beings in their great western palace. After weeks of walking he was almost starving, and then he met an old woman with a beautiful, but mute, daughter. The old woman gave Tchang food and shelter and asked if he would ask the gods to explain why the girl had never been able to speak. After many more weeks of walking, and again near starvation, Tchang met an old man who tended a grove of barren fruit trees. The old man shared his meager supply of food, then asked Tchang to seek an explanation from the gods as to why his trees had stopped yielding fruit.

Tchang continued his journey, but his path was blocked by a raging river. Tchang feared he must abandon his quest, but then a dragon with a beautiful pearl embedded in his forehead appeared and offered to carry him across the river by swimming—for this dragon could not fly. Learning of the young man's journey, the dragon wondered if Tchang could ask the gods to explain why he, the dragon, could not fly.

Across the river Tchang found the palace of the gods and was told he could have three questions answered—but no more. Disappointed, he nevertheless asked the three questions put to him by the trio who helped him. The questions were answered by the gods, and the young man started for home.

When he met the dragon, he told him what the gods had said: "You have to do a good deed for someone. Then you will be able to fly."

The serpent thought for a moment, then removed the precious pearl from his forehead and handed it to Tchang. "You are poor, and kind. I give you the most precious thing I own."

Moved by the dragon's generosity, Tchang continued until he came to the old man with the barren tree. He told him: "Dig in the ground under your tree." When the old man did so, he found several golden jars, each a vessel of pure water. The old man watered his grove, which swiftly blossomed with fruit. In gratitude, the man gave Tchang one of the jars.

When he came again to the house of the woman with the mute daughter, he spoke to her and, much to her surprise, she answered him. Tchang married her and took her home to meet his own mother.

There he found that his despairing mother had cried so much that she had become blind. But when Tchang held the pearl before her, a soft light spilled onto her face and she could see again. That same soft light brought fish to the lake, and with his magic jar Tchang was able to grow many crops in his formerly barren fields. He and his wife lived a happy life of plenty beside the lake. Every year, in the spring, the dragon that had given up his precious pearl came to visit them in a joyful reunion.

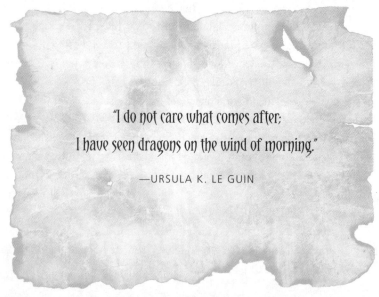

"I do not care what comes after;
I have seen dragons on the wind of morning."

—URSULA K. LE GUIN

Korean Dragons

Korean dragons bear a great resemblance to those of China. They are often depicted as having three toes on their taloned feet, though the greatest of them have four toes. The Korean dragon is sometimes distinguished from other East Asian wyrms in that it can have a very long beard. The dragons of Korea are generally viewed as benign and helpful creatures and have a great deal of influence over water. They are credited with causing rain, and many tales refer to dragons living in rivers and lakes, shallow seas, and even small ponds in the mountains or in fresh-water springs.

Some dragons were venerated for their wisdom, and would offer counsel to kings and sages of Korea. While the possession of pearls was rare among these serpents, some were said to hold one of the precious stones in its foreclaws—always this would be a four-toed dragon, since it possessed a "thumb" to allow it to grasp the treasure.

The Imoogi

Imoogi, or Imugi, are huge serpents with the potential to become dragons. They are snakelike, and according to legend one must be 1,000 years old before it can become a dragon. An Imoogi becomes a true dragon if he attains that advanced age and then catches a Yeouiju, a treasure that falls from heaven. Often that treasure is represented as a virgin maiden, and if she becomes the Imoogi's willing bride he will become a great and honorable dragon.

It is generally considered a sign of good luck to spy an Imoogi, since they are considered benign and helpful, though rarely one can become cruel and villainous.

CHICKEN DRAGONS

The Korean cockatrice is sometimes referred to as a chicken dragon. It is a two-legged dragon with a rooster's head. In fact, the cockatrice also appears in English myth and literature. Shakespeare refers to one in *Twelfth Night*. The cockatrice is the result of an egg laid by a rooster (in itself a pretty neat trick) and then incubated by a serpent. In some depictions, the cockatrice is shown with wings.

Dragons of Japan

The dragons of Japanese mythology are a very mixed bag. Some of them are evil and represent greed, violence, and decay as much as any European type of pestilential wyrm. Others offer various portents, often warning of dire things to come, while still other dragons are beneficent friends of mankind, much like the common dragons of Chinese lore.

In classical Japan, the people believed that their emperors were descendants of dragons, because the very first human ruler of the land, Jimmu Tenno, was said to have been the grandson of a dragon.

Ryujin: God of the Sea

As an island, Japan has always been very dependent upon the surrounding ocean for food and protection from enemies. But the sea is also an ever-present threat to island peoples, and the Japanese people have been very respectful of its awesome power. It seems only fitting that they worshipped such a powerful and magnificent beast as Ryujin, the dragon god. They viewed him as the divine master of the vast ocean surrounding their home.

Ryujin had a huge mouth, capable of swallowing large ships and whales, and when he opened it under water and inhaled he could create great whirlpools on the surface of the water. His scales, claws, horns, and tongue were a beautiful deep blue color. Like many other dragons of Asian (and other) mythos, he was capable of turning himself into a human shape. In this form he could mate with human women and even father children. Indeed, his daughter was the mother of Jimmu Tenno, the first Japanese emperor, so it was said that Ryujin was the ancestor of the entire line of Japanese rulers.

Ryujin dwelt on the ocean floor in a fabulous and bejeweled palace called Ryugu-jo made from white and red coral. The massive abode had four great halls, each devoted to one of the seasons: The winter hall was snowy and white; the spring hall was lined with every blossoming cherry tree; the summer hall was lively with the sound of chirping crickets; and the autumnal hall was brightly colored with stately maple trees in their fall plumage. It was said that if a human spent but one day in Ryujin's splendid hall, that would be the equivalent of 100 years on earth.

The sea god was served by many loyal servants—marine animals including massive turtles, fish both large and small, and jellyfish. He controlled the tides with magical jewels, and while generally a benign deity he could, when angered, send fierce storms to sweep across the sea and bring ruin to ships and low-lying coastal lands. It was also said that no human could look upon the full majesty of this beautiful dragon's body and survive the sight.

THE BONESMASHER

One story about Ryujin illustrates his temper as well as his power. The sea god suffered from an uncomfortable rash, and he learned that the cure required, as a key ingredient, the liver of a monkey. He sent one of his servants, a jellyfish, to bring him the monkey's liver. But when the jellyfish accosted a clever monkey at the seashore, the monkey claimed that its liver was stored in a jar deep in the forest. The monkey offered to go into the woods to retrieve the liver, and the jellyfish let it go. When, not surprisingly, the monkey never returned, the jellyfish was forced to return to its master's palace and report the failure. Ryujin flew into a rage and pulverized the jellyfish so severely that every bone in its body was broken—thus explaining why, to this day, jellyfish have no bones.

A Potent Ally in War

Ryujin's descendant, the Empress Jingo, planned an attack against her peoples' traditional enemy, the Koreans. She had assembled a large fleet to carry her army over the sea to the mainland peninsula of her foes, but she knew that the Koreans also had a large fleet and that they would sail forth to meet the Japanese in a naval battle. Fearing the outcome of the fight, she asked her patron deity, Ryujin, for assistance. The god of the sea obliged by giving her two of his tide stones and instructed her in how to use them.

Jingo and her fleet put to sea and approached Korea. As expected, the Korean fleet sallied forth to meet the ships of Japan. When the two fleets were about to clash, Jingo threw the first of the tide stones over the side of her ship, as far out in the water as she could. This was the low-tide stone, and it caused the tide to recede suddenly, leaving the ships of both fleets stranded on the flat sea bottom. The Japanese warriors, following orders, stayed aboard their vessels while the Koreans, wielding their swords and bearing their shields, scrambled off the ships and onto the sea floor. They started to charge toward the Japanese ships when Jingo cast the second of her magical gems—the high-tide stone. The waters rushed back, refloating the ships but drowning the Korean soldiers who were trapped on the floor of the sea.

Yamata no Orochi

The Orochi was one of the most destructive and fearsome dragons described in any culture. The full name means "big snake of eight branches," and it is quite descriptive of this beast, which was so huge that his body lay across eight hills and eight valleys. Orochi had eight heads at one end and eight massive tails at the other end of his great, grotesque body. Each head had two eyes that glowed as red as winter cherries. With the heads mounted on supple necks, the dragon could see in all directions. His tails lashed through the air so fast that they created a mournful, wailing whistle as they whipped back and forth.

The belly of the beast was swollen and bloody; always demanding he was to be fed. The dragon's back was so broad, and so filthy with dirt, that whole groves of trees had sprouted there. Moss covered the scales over the rest of the vile serpent's form. The dragon was said to live near the foot of Mount Sentsuzan, in Izumo Province near the middle of the largest Japanese island, Honshu. Many valiant warriors had tried to kill the dragon, but none of them had succeeded even in wounding the creature—while each, to a man, had paid for his heroism with his life. Orochi continued to grow fat on human flesh, terrorizing many villages around the province. And each year he had his favorite meal when he compelled the people to offer him a beautiful virgin sacrifice. One family was known for its beautiful and faithful daughters, and seven of them had thus far been given to the dragon. Now their eighth daughter, the only one remaining, had blossomed into young adulthood—and they despaired as they learned that she, too, was destined to be staked out for the monster's unspeakable pleasure.

A Hero Expelled from Heaven

Now, it so happened that a prince named Susanoo was the son of the god of sea and storms. His father had expelled him from their cosmic home because of a trick he had played on his sister, the sun goddess. So Susanoo, in the guise of a man, came to earth and walked the lands of Izumo Province. For a long time he didn't meet any other people, until he came to the River Hi and spotted a pair of chopsticks floating down the stream. Reasoning that they must have come from humans, he followed the bank upstream and found two elderly folk, a man and a woman, weeping inconsolably at the riverbank. A beautiful young girl, also sad and distraught, sat between them.

"Why are you crying?" asked Susanoo. The elders explained that their seven older daughters had all been taken by the dragon Orochi, and now it was time for their eighth daughter to be sacrificed to the monster as well. Susanoo saw that the young girl was indeed very beautiful, and he realized that it would be a great tragedy if she was given to a beast as cruel as the dragon Orochi.

"What is the form of this dragon?" the prince inquired. The parents described his eight awful heads, the massive size of his form, and his insatiable and cruel hunger.

"If I save your daughter, will you give her to me as my wife?" asked Susanoo, to which the disbelieving parents readily assented.

"So it shall be," said the prince. At once he used magic, changing the girl—much to the astonishment of her parents—into a fine-toothed comb, which he tucked into his long hair for safekeeping. Susanoo then instructed the parents to brew eight large vats of potent rice wine, and then build a fence with eight gates around their home. They were to place one vat of wine on a platform inside of each of the gates and await the coming of Orochi.

This they did, and when the dragon slithered toward their home to claim his sacrifice, he was drawn to the strong scent of the wine. Each of his heads went to a different vat and he drank greedily until all the vats were empty. The dragon collapsed on the ground, thoroughly drunk.

Now Susanoo approached. He bore a sword of sharp and sturdy steel, and he swiftly cut the heads from the dragon, and then proceeded to cut the body into pieces. So much blood was shed that the River Hi ran red for a very long time. But the people were freed from the menace of the dragon, and Susanoo had won for himself a beautiful bride.

O-Gon-Cho

The O-Gon-Cho was a white dragon that lived deep in a lake near Yamashiro on the island of Kyoto. The dragon would stay below the water for the most part, and for decades the people tended to forget that it existed. Yet, unfortunately, about every fifty years the dragon would rise from the waters and appear as a giant bird with golden feathers. It was a beautiful sight as the sun reflected from its wonderful plumage. But when the bird spread its beak, it uttered a terrifying, howling wail that sounded like all the torments of the underworld. This noise revealed the beast's true nature, for the coming of the O-Gon-Cho never failed to precede some disaster, such as earthquake, famine, or disease.

The Dragon of Mano Pond

One of the good dragons of Japanese mythology is said to have lived in this large, deep pond—a body of water more like a lake than a pond. This dragon relied upon water for all of his great powers, but even so he liked to emerge into the air on a sunny day so that he could bask in the warm rays. When he emerged from the lake, he did so in the form of a small snake, slithering up to a flat rock and stretching himself luxuriously.

One day while he was thus enjoying the sun, however, a winged gnome, called a tengu, swooped down from the sky and snatched up what it thought was a snake. The dragon was so startled by the abduction that he was not able to wriggle free. The tengu, for its part, was surprised and frustrated that it could not simply crush the snake in its powerful, taloned hands. After all, it had killed many snakes this way in the past! But of course, this snake was really a dragon.

Furious, the tengu flew back to its mountain lair with the snake-dragon still clutched in its grasp. As the dragon had dried out from the long exposure to the air, he had lost his magical powers—which, of course, were based in water—and was unable to prevent the tengu from stuffing him into a small crack in a sheer cliff on the mountainside. The tengu blocked up the hole with a wedge of rock, and flew away, leaving the dragon helpless to change shape or to wriggle out of the hole.

Some time later the tengu returned with another prisoner, this one a pious monk. The flying gnome pulled the wedge of rock out of the way and stuffed the monk into the same crack where the snake-dragon was held. As soon as the tengu flew away again, the dragon surprised the monk by speaking, asking the man how he had come to be captured.

"I was fetching water from the stream," the monk replied, holding up his jug. "And just as I rose to return to my home that creature swooped down and snatched me."

"Do you have water now?" asked the dragon, to which the monk replied that he did.

"If you will pour that water upon me," explained the dragon, "my powers will be restored and I will be able to fly us out of here and back to safety."

With nothing to lose, the monk agreed, and when he poured his water on the snake the creature grew into his true form, bursting out the wedge that held them inside the crack. The wingless dragon could fly with ease, and he willingly bore the monk back down from the heights to deposit him safely beside his home.

"Are you going back to your pond?" asked the monk, who knew the story of the dragon's home.

"Soon," said the dragon, with a baleful look at the sky. "But first I have a tengu to find." Only when the dragon had his revenge did he return to Mano Pond and slip gratefully beneath the waves.

THE TENGU

In Japanese art, the tengu is sometimes depicted as a bird and sometimes as a dog-like creature. Its dominant feature is its nose, and it is sometimes shown simply as a human figure with an outsized nose.

The Temple of the Dragon Garden

A faithful monk lived and worshipped at a beautiful temple. Every day he went into the garden to perform his mystical chants, and one day he noticed a man who came to listen to him with great reverence. The monk befriended the man, offering him food and drink, and the man graciously thanked him. When the monk asked where the man came from, he confided that he was in fact a dragon, not a man; but he took human form because it made it easier for him to come into the temple, and he dearly loved to hear the monk's chant.

The two became fast friends, and their friendship—between a monk and a dragon!—grew famous throughout Japan. For many years, as the monk aged and the dragon did not, the two spent every afternoon together, one chanting, the other listening and meditating to the beautiful, rhythmic sound.

Unfortunately, there came a time when all of Japan sweltered under a terrible drought. Fields and streams dried up, crops failed, and even the fish seemed to flee away from the island's shores. Unable to think of anything else he could do, the emperor of Japan summoned the monk who was known to be friends with a dragon. The emperor told the monk that he must command his friend the dragon to bring rain. If the monk failed to carry out the emperor's orders, he would be forever exiled from Japan.

When the monk returned to the temple, he told the dragon of the emperor's command. Although he, like all wise and faithful men, knew that dragons had great power over water, he did not even know if his friend, the dragon, was capable of answering the ruler's demand.

"I can cause rain to fall," the dragon admitted sadly. "But it will be a breach of my role, for I am not the dragon who rules over rain. I will make it rain in three days' time, but I shall have to pay with my life."

The monk did not want the dragon to die, and he offered to leave Japan instead. But neither of them could bear the suffering they saw throughout the land, and the dragon insisted that he would, in fact, bring forth rain. He only asked that his friend bury him with honor, and then go to three places and in each erect a temple to the dragon's memory.

The grieving monk agreed, and his friend, taking his true form as a dragon, flew away. In three days' time it began to rain, and soon the fields were fertile again and the streams flowed with water. But the great dragon, as he had predicted, was slain for his disobedience, and his body was left at the gate of the monk's temple. In sadness, the monk buried the body of his friend and built a temple on that spot, a place that would be forever known as the Temple of the Dragon Garden.

Then the monk journeyed to the places the dragon had designated and built the Temple of the Dragon Mind, the Temple of the Dragon Heaven, and the Temple of the Dragon King. For the rest of his days, the monk traveled from one of these temples to another, and in each he chanted prayers in the memory of his friend, the dragon.

CHAPTER 5

DRAGONS
of India and South Asia

ike the peoples of many other early civilizations, the earliest cultures of South Asia created mythologies that imagined deities as bringers of rain and sunshine, fertility and birth—as well as the hazards of storm, lightning, famine, and cold. It is quite possible that the more tropical and rainier climate of India, which is home to many more varieties of snakes than are in the Fertile Crescent, encouraged the mythology of ancient India and its surrounding realms to create dragon myths that imagined a snake-bodied serpent to symbolize many of these godly attributes.

The common serpent-god (and serpent-demon) of these cultural histories was the nāga, a being with the body of a snake but often the head—

or even the head and torso—of a human. Nāgas were generally imbued with great supernatural powers, and the most fearsome snake of them all—the cobra—was often linked, with its hood and venomous bite, to the image of the mighty nāga.

These nāgas were often regarded as demigods, and they varied considerably in temperament and attitudes toward mankind. Some were said to have dwelt like regal monarchs in great palaces beneath the sea or in castles that floated in the clouds. Others lived more like beasts, in dark caverns and ancient ruins. Often the nāgas were said to have great magical powers and could take on human form, which often terminated when the nāga mysteriously disappeared into a hole in the ground or dived into the sea and did not resurface.

The images and legends of the nāga predate the two great religions, Hinduism and Buddhism, that arose in this part of the world. In many early civilizations and proto-civilizations, snake worship formed a key element of belief systems. Both of the major Eastern religions, as they took shape and evolved, incorporated nāgas into their mythology.

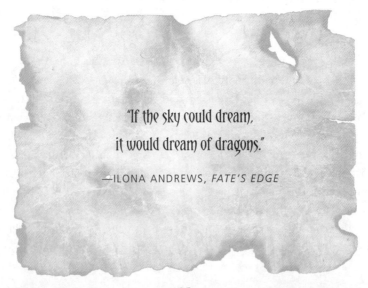

"If the sky could dream,
it would dream of dragons."

—ILONA ANDREWS, *FATE'S EDGE*

Earliest Nāgas

Nāgas (and in their female form, nāgis or nāginis, which are very beautiful) are said to be descended directly from the creator gods Kadru and Kasyapa and are directly related to Vishnu, the greatest god of all. In these legends, nāgas originally dwelt on the surface of the world, but they became so numerous that the god Brahma relegated them to regions under the earth's surface. Because the nāgas possessed such great power, including the ability to change shape between human and snake form, the god also commanded them to bite only those who were truly evil—though they could also bite someone who was fated to die prematurely.

Most of the nāgas departed to the undersea realm of Bhagavati, though others reputedly lived underground in the land called Nāgaloka. In both places they dwelt in fabulous palaces, surrounded by furnishings and possessions bedecked with fabulous jewels. Nāgas in their true form had a human head and often a man or woman's torso and arms but a serpentine body, very much like that of a huge snake. All nāgas and nāgis possessed power that humans could only imagine.

Legend claimed that the race of nāgas was ruled by a king named Ananta-Shesha, who protected and honored the god Vishnu. Ananta-Shesha's subjects wielded great power over water, such as rivers, lakes, oceans, and wells.

Classes of Nāgas

Early Indian mythology broke the nāga classes down into four distinct types, each of which had its own area of power and responsibility.

1. **HEAVENLY NĀGAS:** These powerful, supernatural creatures were the guardians of the lofty palaces of the gods. In some tales, heavenly nāgas actually used their own bodies, or the cobra hoods of their head, to support the immense weight of the palace. The myth of the nāga Shesha, recounted later in this chapter, describes how that nāga supported the entire world on his head! These celestial beings were viewed as essentially benign, but aloof and proud, and deserving of considerable respect.

2. **DIVINE NĀGAS:** Divine nāgas had great power over water, especially water as it existed in the sky. Divine nāgas could create and control clouds, steering them with their breath and directing the clouds to drop rain where the nāgas desired. They could control temperatures to make it snow when they wanted to. Divine nāgas were cherished by farmers because their life-giving rains were necessary to ensure fertile crops. Divine nāgas, too, were deserving of respect, and some legends suggest they would cause draught and starvation if they felt insulted or unappreciated.

3. **EARTHLY NĀGAS:** These nāgas also had power over water, but primarily water that made its way along and through the ground, through rivers, creeks, drains, and outlets. The nāgas dwelt in the water and served as divine dredges, clearing out blockages and keeping channels deep enough so that water could continue to flow. Like the other nāgas, they expected devotion and offerings from lesser beings such as humans.

4. **HIDDEN NĀGAS:** These hidden nāgas guarded treasures. They most commonly dwelt in caves or underwater palaces, but some tales describe them as inhabiting ancient ruins and abandoned temples. Treasures most cherished by nāgas included gems and jewels, but also unique items forged by gods and given to (or stolen by) the nāgas for safekeeping. They were known to be territorial and possessive—both traits that make for good guardians—and people who dared to delve under the ground would do well to honor the hidden nāgas.

SNAKE WORSHIP

Snake worship is, of course, not unique to Asia. In Crete, excavations at the ancient site of Knossos have found evidence for worship of a snake goddess among the Minoan people, who flourished around 1600 B.C. In Africa, there was a cult of the python during the first part of the seventeenth century. And in America, there is a tradition of snake handling among some Pentecostal Christian sects.

Notable Early Nāgas

Three of these early nāga demigods play an important role in the Hindu myths of creation: Shesha (sometimes called Ananta), Vasuki, and Taksaka.

Shesha

Shesha was the king of the nāgas and one of the original beings in the cosmos. He dwelt upon the surface of the universal ocean, the place that supported all existence. Shesha's broad hood supported Vishnu himself, and thus the entire world. He was said to be the oldest nāga, the first of a thousand born to Kadru and Kasyapa. In some versions of the myth he is depicted with five heads; others portray him as having many thousands of heads growing from his vast, coiling body.

Many of Shesha's siblings turned out to be cruel and hurtful, and they delighted in causing pain and death among other beings of the cosmos. When his siblings, especially his brother, turned to torturing their sisters, Shesha grew disgusted and left his family to float weightless in the atmosphere above the firmament. Some say that he drifted through the sky amid the highest peaks of the Himalayas. He meditated and inflicted punishments upon himself in an effort to atone for the villainy of his brothers.

Eventually Shesha had thrashed and tortured himself to such an extent that all the soft tissue of his body—flesh, skin, and muscle—atrophied and left him only as a skeleton.

The god Brahma took pity upon Shesha's great suffering and asked the great nāga to make a request of the god. Shesha's request was humble: He asked merely to hold his mind intact so that he could continue seeking forgiveness for the sins of his clan. The god granted the request and then asked a favor of his own, one that Shesha would be bound to perform.

Brahma asked the great nāga to take himself beneath the still-unstable firmament of the world, where with his great size and strength he could support and stabilize the entire earth with his broad hood. Shesha agreed to this request and slipped under the world to hold it upon his hood. There are those who believe that he still supports it today.

Vasuki

Vasuki was a huge nāga, many miles long. In ancient myth he was hailed as being an important part of the creation of the world. Before that world was created, the universe was an ocean of magic material, sometimes described as "cosmic milk." It contained the building blocks of life and existence, but it had no form, and without form, life could not take place.

The gods and demons together approached the huge nāga Vasuki and asked him to churn the milk with his body and thicken it so the mighty beings could extract from it the essence of immortality. Vasuki agreed, and so the gods and demons entwined him around a tall mountain—often named Mount Mandar. The gods pulled on one end of the huge nāga and the demons pulled on the other, which caused the mountain to spin back and forth in the cosmic ocean, churning the milk to the material that became the substance of life.

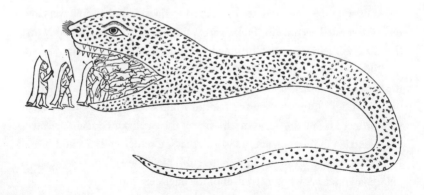

Taksaka

Taksaka was another great nāga of the early era. He ruled over a large realm of nāgas in the Khandava Forest until a consortium of his enemies, led by the brothers Pandava, drove him from his palace into the wilderness. With his nāga followers, Taksaka created a new city called Takshasila, where he ruled over his fellow nāgas and brooded about the great injustice that had been done to him.

Finally, after many years had passed, Taksaka determined to take his vengeance. For his target he selected the grandson of one of the Pandava brothers, a king known as Parikshit. The nāga poisoned the king's food, causing the descendant of the Pandavas to collapse into writhing agony and linger, very near to dying. The king's followers sought help from a Kasyapa priest, a man reputed to be the only one who knew a cure for the venom of a nāga. However, Taksaka had anticipated the request and had already bribed the priest to make sure he would not offer his aid to the suffering king. As a result, Parikshit died in great pain.

Naturally, the dead king's son, Prince Janamejaya, was enraged by this assassination. He mustered his men and formed a great army, which he hurled against the nāgas in their city of Takshasila. The nāgas were individually powerful, but the humans far outnumbered them. The prince's men burst through the walls and razed the city, once more driving Taksaka and his followers into the wilderness. This time the human army pursued them so aggressively that the nāgas were driven out of the kingdom, and had no land of their own.

They became bandits, and terrorized travelers who sought to reach the new city Janamejaya had erected on the site of Takshasila. Janamejaya, now king, was infuriated by the banditry and sent his army forth again with orders to wipe the nāgas off the face of the earth. Once again defeated, Taksaka tried to retreat from the world, seeking refuge with the god Indra. Before he escaped, however, he and his sub-chiefs were captured and taken before Janamejaya, who ordered all of the nāgas executed.

It was then that a Brahmin sage, Astika, spoke up, pleading for peace and forgiveness so eloquently that the king changed his mind. The nāgas were released and allowed to return to Takshasila, where for the remainder of time they dwelt side by side with mankind, in lasting peace.

Garuda: Bane of the Nāgas

Kasyapa the god had thirteen wives. One, Kadru, was the mother of the nāgas. Kadru desired many offspring, and so the god blessed her with a thousand eggs, each of which hatched and grew into a nāga prince. Another of Kasyapa's wives, Vinata, wanted to have only a small number of children but wanted them to be imbued with terrible power. As a result of this wish, Kasyapa gave her two eggs, each of which she protected for 500 years. When they hatched, one of them gave birth to the mighty eagle-king known as Garuda.

Garuda was a mighty and beautiful being. He had the body of a brightly colored eagle, brilliant with plumage of gold and green feathers. His wings were red, and he had four human arms growing out of his torso. He had the head of a bird, but his face was that of a man, a handsome visage that appeared to be made out of gold.

Vinata made a foolish bet with her sister-wife, Kadru. The stakes were high: The loser was to become the slave of the winner. Vinata bet that Uchaishravas, the divine horse, was fully white in color. Kadru claimed the horse was white but the tail was black. The horse was in fact fully white, but Kadru convinced her sons—who were black snakes—to twist themselves around the tail to make it appear black. After persuasion and threats from Kadru, the sons agreed to perform the deception. The tail looked black, so Vinata lost the bet. Not content with possessing the goddess, Kadru demanded that Vinata's son, the eagle-king, become her slave as well, and Vinata agreed to the cruel request. Though he was willing to perform the role set for him by his mother, Garuda despised the nāgas for what they demanded of the goddess, and this enmity would last throughout eternity.

Eventually, the eagle-king determined to change his fate. He asked of Kadru what he must do in order for the nāgas to agree to Vinata's freedom. The snake-people declared that if Garuda could bring them *amrita*, an elixir that granted immortality, they would release Vinata from her bet. The eagle-king's hatred for the nāgas raged at fever pitch, but he greatly desired his mother's freedom. He managed to obtain amrita and brought it to the nāgas. However, once they agreed that Vinata was freed from the pledge of servitude, Garuda spilled the elixir so that the nāgas were unable to attain their cherished goal of eternal life. Far from being content with this result, Garuda became the sworn enemy of the nāgas and all other snakes, and devoted his own existence to killing—and often eating—them whenever he could.

THE POWER OF *AMRITA*

The *amrita* sought by the nāgas was a marvelous drink extracted from the cosmic milk that lay at the origin of all being. It was the potion that granted the gods themselves immortality and was first created when the original (nearly) eternal life spans of the gods began to wane. Sensing the danger, they used the nāga Vasuki to churn the ocean to extract the amrita, as well as many other useful and wonderful substances, from the material of original creation.

Garuda Tricked

It came to pass that Matali, who was the charioteer of the god Indra, wanted to marry his daughter Gunakesi to the grandson of a mighty nāga named Aryaka. The nāga replied that she would have been delighted to arrange the match with her grandson, Sumukha—who was indeed a very handsome man in human form. But Aryaka could not make the promise because the eagle-king Garuda had made known his intention to kill and devour Sumukha. (In fact, Garuda had already slain Sumukha's father, Aryaka's son.)

Perhaps, Aryaka suggested slyly, Matali could find a way to protect Sumukha from the eagle-king, thus allowing him to marry the charioteer's daughter. Matali agreed readily and persuaded Indra and Vishnu to allow Sumukha to drink a swallow of amrita. The handsome young nāga drank the magical liquid, which rendered him invulnerable to the eagle-king's attack, and the two young lovers were married and lived a long, happy life.

NECTAR OF THE GODS

The word *amrita* has the same root as the Greek word for ambrosia, and in fact has much the same meaning as well.

Vritra

One of the oldest dragon myths in the world comes to us from India and describes a battle between two of the mightiest gods in the Hindu pantheon. One of these gods was Indra, deity of warriors and benign of nature. Indra, one of the primary deities in the Hindu pantheon, was the bringer of rain, which was universally recognized as the source of life and nourishment.

One of Indra's potent enemies—perhaps his greatest foe—was the dragon Vritra. This serpent was so vast in extent that he sprawled across huge mountaintops. Vritra was, among other things, the god of drought, and in his swollen belly he held all the waters of the world. Indra knew he would have to slay the dragon in order to release those waters, and thus fertility, upon the world.

By some accounts the two had fought many battles throughout the eras before mankind. Indra rode a chariot that was formed from the sun and used thunderbolts as his arrows. But Vritra was so vast and supple that he was able to encircle Indra in his coils. At one point, Vritra actually swallowed Indra, only spitting him out when confronted by the rest of the gods.

Finally the ruling god, Vishnu, ordered that the fighting between them cease, decreeing that neither could attack the other with anything that was formed of iron, wood, or stone. Nor could they attack with anything that was wet or dry, nor could they do battle during the day or the night. This seemed to set the matter to rest, but it did not solve the problem of allowing rain to fall or rivers to flow across the surface of the world.

But eventually Indra saw his chance to attack: Vritra lolled along the shore of the great ocean late one afternoon, as the sun was just about to set. With the aid of Vishnu (who was not a neutral observer after all) Indra concealed himself in the foam of the surf, which was judged to be neither wet nor dry. As the sun set, so that it was neither day nor night, Indra flew upon his enemy in the guise of foam, strangling Vritra and ultimately slaying the mighty dragon.

As the serpent died, his swollen body burst open and water flooded across the land, bringing the rivers to life. The vapors of liquid rose into clouds, like a great herd of cattle in the skies. The clouds spread through the heavens, and they quickly started to release rain.

Karkotaka

A powerful nāga king, Karkotaka, lived in a forest near the kingdom of Nishada. Legends claim that Karkotaka had angered one of the most powerful sages of the Hindu pantheon, Narada, by cheating him in a game of chance. Narada knew powerful magic, and he placed a curse of immobility upon the nāga king. This curse bound Karkotaka to the ground in his forest kingdom. The sage promised that the curse would last forever unless one man—a monarch named King Nala—came to the nāga's aid.

King Nala, in fact, was ruler of the Nishada Kingdom that was close to Karkotaka's forest in ancient India. He was a very handsome and capable man, known for his great skill at horsemanship and, oddly enough, for his wonderful ability as a chef. The princess Damayanti, of the nearby Vidarbha Kingdom, chose Nala to be her husband, and the people of both lands celebrated. Despite his known weakness for gambling, Nala was a good and steadfast man, and he was determined to be a worthy husband and king.

After a few years, however, Nala began to fail in his efforts to be a worthy king. The demon Kali took possession of him and caused him to lose his entire kingdom to his brother over a single throw of dice. Shamed and defeated, Nala fled his kingdom and took shelter in the forest.

Soon a great fire began, consuming all of the trees in the forest, turning the land to a wasteland of ash. Nala, retreating from the flames, heard a loud voice calling for help and came upon the mighty nāga, still held in place by the curse placed upon him. The fallen king at once tried to help, and as soon as his hands touched the nāga, Karkotaka broke free of the curse. The two escaped together and became good friends.

But the god Indra spoke to the nāga and warned him that the demon Kali still lurked within his human comrade. Karkotaka made a plan to help Nala. He asked the fugitive king to walk away from him; Nala counted his footsteps out loud as he walked. On the tenth step, the nāga struck—he bit Nala and injected his body with a venom that caused his body to shrivel and become deformed, so that he was no longer recognizable as the handsome man he had been.

Nala was angered by this apparent betrayal by a comrade he had viewed as a friend, but Karkotaka explained to him his plan. He told Nala of a place where he could go to gain enlightenment, studying under a master in a nearby kingdom. This opportunity would not be available to him if he was recognized as a king—hence the disguise. Once he gained enlightenment, the demon Kali would be expelled and Nala would have control of his own destiny. Then Karkotaka gave Nala a cloak and told him that when he put it on he would return to his normal form.

With this generous act the nāga disappeared from the tale, but it is said that the king attained enlightenment, returned to his normal appearance, and went back to live a long and prosperous life with his beautiful bride.

A NĀGA'S LEGACY IN THE MODERN WORLD

Even today, there are many temples in India, including one very famous, as well as a range of hills all named after the nāga Karkotaka.

Paravatakṣha

Paravataksha was a nāga king who possessed a mighty sword forged by gods, a weapon lost by its maker during a heavenly war. Though his body was a snake, the nāga's torso was that of a man, and it was with his human hands that he could wield the weapon. It was said that the wielder of the sword would never know defeat and could cause earthquakes merely by smashing the blade on the ground.

Nevertheless, the nāga was a peaceful being. He lived in a palace beneath a solitary asoka tree. Its entrance was a water-filled cave that was magically concealed from view during the daylight so that it resembled a damp patch of mud. But the entrance could be discovered at sunset when it became the favored landing place of a pair of beautiful swans.

One day a sorcerer was abroad in the forest. He had learned of the nāga's sword through magic spells and potent drugs. The sorcerer corrupted many a young man to learn the secrets of its existence and the general area where it could be found. He had also learned of the swans, which revealed the location of the magical cave mouth. He desperately craved the sword, but he knew it could only be captured by one who had the aid of great heroes on his quest. As the years went by and the sorcerer could not find the nāga's cave, he despaired of ever fulfilling his greedy quest. Finally he collapsed in despair and began to slowly starve.

In this wretched state he was discovered by a king who happened to be traveling through the forest with a band of heroic fighters. The king asked the sorcerer how he came to be here alone, and when he was told the sorcerer's quest, the king offered the aid of his party to help the old man attain his life's goal. It happened that the king's men had seen the swans landing just the night before, and so they led the sorcerer to the spot— which was indeed marked by the lofty height of a solitary asoka tree.

The king and the sorcerer made their plan: The sorcerer would use his magic to reveal the mouth of the cave, and then chant an incantation that would daze the snake so that it could not fight effectively. The king's men were then to attack, kill the nāga, and steal the sword.

The swans landed at dusk, and the sorcerer advanced. He cast enchanted mustard seeds onto the pond, causing the water to fall away and revealing the entrance to the cave that led to the palace. An earthquake shook the ground and terrible thunder crashed from the skies as the nāga king, still unseen by his attackers, beat the ground with his enchanted blade. The king and his men felt terrible fear, but the sorcerer advanced, casting a spell to hold the snake at bay so it could be killed. He continued his chant, and the party of attackers crept closer to the cave.

Suddenly a beautiful young nymph emerged from the cave, bedecked in jewels, with a haunting, hypnotic pair of wide dark eyes. She turned those eyes upon the sorcerer, and it was as though a spear had been driven through his heart. So enchanting was her beauty that the snake-bane chant died upon his lips and he stared, mute, at the most lovely creature he had ever seen.

In the next instant she vanished and the nāga king himself reared up from the hole. His eyes blazed with fire, and the great sword gleamed silver in his mighty hand. With one blow he killed the sorcerer, and then turned his fearsome gaze upon the king and his would-be heroic warriors. The nāga burned with rage, and the hot glowing coals of his furious eyes caused all of the men to fall blind. With a curse as loud as thunder, he deafened them. The king and his companions fled the place in terror, each of them running in a different direction. Since they could neither see nor hear each other, each man was condemned to wander alone for many months until finally the curse wore off and they returned, much chastened, to the kingdom.

Dragons of Buddhist Mythology

The nāga is a universal presence in Buddhist traditions as well as those of the Hindus. They are viewed as wise and powerful beings, often merging with tales of more traditional dragons. In Tibet, the nāga is often hailed as a guardian of treasure dwelling in lakes or underground streams, while in China the nāga is commonly associated with the Chinese dragon, or lung.

One tale tells of a nāga in human form who declared to the Buddha that he wished to become a monk. Despite his manlike guise, the nāga was told that only a human could attain enlightenment or serve as a monk. The Buddha then explained to the nāga how he could still live a virtuous life, thus increasing the chances that when he was reborn he would return to the world as a human.

Another story relates how an eight-year-old female nāga was able to change her shape into a male human and immediately achieve enlighten-ment. This story would seem to contradict the previous bit of mythology and may have been created as a means to underscore that many priests and monks believed only males could achieve enlightenment.

There are frequent mentions of nāgas in the Buddhist holy writings. Often they are mentioned as followers who come to hear the Buddha speak. The Buddha and the nāgas almost invariably treat each other with great, mutual respect.

BUDDHIST NĀGAS

In the Buddhist tradition, the nāga is usually portrayed as having the head or face of a man and the body of a long snake, such as a king cobra. Some of the nāgas have multiple heads, while others have hoods like that of a cobra; still others can change shape into that of a human. (This is a trait they share with many East Asian dragons.)

Mucalinda: Protector of the Buddha

A famous story tells of a nāga, Mucalinda, who was king of a splendid realm under a great lake. After the Buddha attained his enlightenment beneath the Bodhi tree, he was journeying through a great forest, stopping frequently for extended periods of meditation. So rapt was he in his musings that he did not notice that a terrible storm was approaching. The nāga king was aware, however, and he emerged from his lair and coiled himself around the tree beneath which the Buddha sat. The nāga raised his hooded head and stretched it overhead, protecting the great guru from the storm. The fierce storm lasted for seven days, and the nāga remained in position for the entire time. After the storm had passed, Mucalinda shifted into his human form so that he could bow before the Buddha. Filled with joy, the nāga took snake form once again and returned to his palace. This episode is commonly portrayed in the art of South Asia and Southeast Asia; Mucalinda is often pictured with seven heads.

The Nāga Apalala

This story is widely known throughout the Buddhist world and was often told to children because of the strength of its moral lesson. The nāga is described as having the head of a man, though his mouth is studded with sharp teeth. His torso is also like a human's, and though he lacks wings he is a powerful flier. His body is serpentine, and he has a long, lashing tail. A dorsal fin extends down his back and along the length of his tail. This fin allows him to maneuver in air or water with great dexterity. He has two legs and feet that are clawed like the talons of a great bird of prey.

The nāga Apalala is said to have lived in the Swat River valley in what is now Pakistan. He was a huge water dragon, capable of controlling the rain and the flow of the river. His nature was mostly benign, and the farmers credited him with holding at bay other, evil dragons who would try to create rainstorms, floods, and droughts. Because they were happy to have his protection, the peoples of the valley for many years paid a great tribute in grain to Apalala, and this pleased him mightily.

But Apalala was so effective at preventing floods and droughts that the people began to take his blessings for granted. Many of them stopped leaving the tributes of grain, and Apalala became angered by this neglect. To punish the farmers for their lack of faith, he brought a powerful flood that swept down the valley one year, and in the next he withdrew the waters so that all the fields withered and dried under a terrible drought. Relishing his power and his vengeance, the nāga continued to torment the people in this way, so that they could not dependably grow their crops.

Finally, the Buddha himself came to the Swat valley. He had compassion for the people who were starving because of the nāga's spite, and so he sought out Apalala and spoke to him. The Buddha was able to convince Apalala that it was wrong to make the humans suffer because of what he was doing, and in this wise counsel the nāga saw the error of his ways.

Apalala converted and became a Buddhist. He promised to stop his torment of the farmers, though he did ask that he be given a large tribute once every dozen years. The people were grateful for his beneficence and granted his request. Every twelve years Apalala sends heavy rains to the valley so that there is extra grain, and the farmers give this surplus to the nāga in gratitude for his kindness and mercy.

THE NĀGA LEGEND AS LITERARY INSPIRATION

Rudyard Kipling, in his story of a heroic mongoose "Rikki-Tikki-Tavi," created two mighty cobras as villainous adversaries to the hero. The names of these snakes, Nag and Nāgina, were clearly inspired by tales from the nāga legends of India. The snakes are potent enemies, menacing a British family living in India, and the brave mongoose acts as the traditional hero in this adventure story.

Nāgas of Southeast Asia

Nāga legends are common in Thailand, Cambodia, Laos, Vietnam, Malaysia, and Indonesia. Like the nāgas of the Indian subcontinent, these draconic archetypes are mixtures of human and snake. Some are seagoing, while many are said to dwell territorially in specific rivers or lakes. Specific aspects of their appearance vary from place to place: Malay sailors historically believed that nāgas were dragons with many heads, while people in Laos frequently pictured them as water serpents with sharp, hooked beaks.

Phaya Nāga

This powerful serpent lives in the Mekong River and is most associated with the countries of Laos and Thailand. The nāga dates back to the earliest kings of Laos, and was said to guard Vientiane, the capital city. Phaya Nāga is described in detail in historical accounts of Anouvong, the last king of Vientiane. This nāga is said to have been a protector of the entire nation, not just the capital city.

According to many believers, Phaya Nāga still lives in the Mekong River, and its existence is proven by a unique natural phenomenon known as the Nāga Fireballs. These are glowing orbs about the size of chicken eggs that rise from a stretch of the Mekong River in Thailand, usually about the time of the end of the monsoon season. Although the fireballs have a scientific explanation involving the fermentation of river sediments and other such mundane considerations, these explanations are of no import to many of the local people. In fact, the glowing orbs have led people to hold festivals along the mighty river. And when attendees see the Nāga Fireballs float into the air, sometimes thousands at a time, it is safe to say that the people prefer to believe the Nāga Fireballs are the enchanted eggs of Phaya Nāga.

POLITICAL INTRIGUE IN THE SERPENT LEGEND

An interesting legend uses the story of Phaya Nāga to symbolize Laos, and the Garuda eagle-king—earlier described as a mortal enemy of nāgas—to represent the neighboring nation of Siam (now Thailand.) The two nations have a long history of rivalry and distrust. This is one of many examples of serpent myths used to underscore actual circumstances existing in human societies.

A Nāga of Cambodian Lore: Ḳaliya

Ancient Cambodian culture used a great nāga as part of the creation myth of the people of that nation. The daughter of a nāga king, Kaliya, married a mighty Brahmana named Kaundinya. Their offspring became the Cambodian people, and many of those people still say that they are "born from the nāga."

Kaliya's Survival

Like so many tales of legendary nāgas, the role of the nāga-killer Garuda plays a prominent part in the story of Kaliya's life and his rise to greatness. When Garuda the eagle-king engaged upon his quest to exterminate nāgas from the world, Kaliya, a mighty and venomous nāga, fled to the Yamuna River where he sought shelter. He poisoned the waters so much that, for miles in both directions, the river boiled and bubbled with toxins, killing even the trees that grew along the banks of that river—all except for one tall Kadamba tree, which still survived, its broad limbs spreading over the flowing water of the toxic river.

The Yamuna River is a major tributary of the Ganges, in northern India. For part of its length it flows through the province of Vrindivan, where a powerful yogi lived. This yogi had placed a curse upon the eagle-king, barring him from the province. When Kaliya was forced to flee the deadly bird, he chose for his refuge the section of the Yamuna river where the curse prevented Garuda from following.

One of the primary Hindu gods, Krishna—who often is depicted as a playful youth and, even though he was one of the most powerful deities in the cosmos, was fond of making mischief—was playing ball with a group of boys along the bank of the Yamuna River. Krishna climbed into the long Kadamba tree and reached out over the river to try and catch the ball. Instead, he missed it and fell into the water.

Kaliya Is Surprised

Immediately the great nāga rose up, 110 hooded heads looming above the water. He spewed poison from every head onto the boy floating in the water, then wrapped his serpentine body around Krishna's body and dragged him under the surface, intending to drown and devour him.

But the nāga could not subdue the mighty god. Krishna's body began to grow until he became so large that even the huge nāga could not hold him. The nāga struck at the god with his many heads, but Krishna turned away every attack. Finally Krishna grew angry and began to stomp upon the nāga's heads. He brought the weight of the entire universe within him, bore Kaliya to the bottom of the river, and began crushing the life out of him.

But Kaliya had many wives, at least seven and perhaps as many as a hundred, and they very much adored their nāga lord. All of the wives swam through the river water and gathered around Krishna, praying to him with their palms pressed together like true supplicants. Kaliya, knowing his cause was lost, joined in their pleas and honored the god with acknowledgment of his greatness. He submitted to Krishna and vowed that he would never more seek to harm those who came within his sights. So Krishna allowed the nāga to go free. It is said that the nāga swam to the ocean and made his way far out into the Pacific, where he formed a new nāga kingdom and lived a long and prosperous life, far from the reach of the murderous eagle-king.

Nāgas of Malaysia and Indonesia

Malay sailors long believed that nāgas were water dragons with multiple heads. Other people, notably on the island of Java, worshiped nāgas as powerful demigods that dwelt in a hidden underground palace filled with great treasures. Some nāgas are depicted, particularly in Indonesia, similarly to Chinese dragons— that is, they possess four legs and clawed feet. They were excellent swimmers and sometimes stole the fish from fisherman's nets. They cherished natural beauty, particularly the lotus flower.

Throughout the lands of Southeast Asia, nāgas fulfill the universal role of the dragon, or great serpent, in nearly every culture's ancestral myths. In the Philippine Islands, dating back before the arrival of the Spaniards, nāgas were used to adorn the hilts of the swords used by the islanders.

The Nāga of Sri Gumum

The legend is still told today about the forming of Lake Chini, the second largest lake in Malaysia. Aboriginal settlers moved southward down the long, slender peninsula of Malaya. Thick jungle covered most of the land, but settlers finally discovered a region of savannah where they would be able to farm enough to settle. The people built houses and began to clear the grasslands so that they could plant their crops.

One day, as the settlement neared completion and the first round of crops had been planted, a strange old woman emerged from the jungle and hobbled toward them, leaning upon a stick to support her frail body.

"Why are you here?" she demanded. "I am the owner of this place, and you need my permission to live here!"

The people were taken aback. "We are sorry, lady—we did not know this place was yours," said the chieftain. "Please accept our humblest apology."

He went on to offer her food and drink, while other people brought her a chair so that she could sit in comfort. Because they treated her with respect, she told them that she would give them permission to stay there. As she rose to leave, however, she thrust her stick into the ground, where it stuck, jutting into the air.

"For as long as you live here, you must leave my stick in this place," she warned them, before she suddenly departed.

Not long after this, however, black clouds shrouded the sky and thunder rang from the clouds. The storm pressed lower, and lightning lashed the surrounding forest, then struck one of the houses in the small settlement. The villagers panicked, running every which way, trying to avoid the fury of the storm. In the panic, confused by the driving rain, one man ran into the stick the old woman had planted; he pulled it out and cast it aside as he stumbled on.

Immediately, water spurted from the ground where the stick had been, quickly rising to flood the center of the village, still churning forth to spread across the fields. The stick, meanwhile, became a great snake with the head of a man. He roared his anger at them, and the last of the people fled into the jungle. Their village was now subsumed beneath a lake, and from that time on the lake was known as the lair of a great nāga.

THE NĀGA AS TOURIST ATTRACTION

Lake Chini is now the site of considerable development and is one of the more popular inland tourist destinations in the southern Malayan peninsula. A large sign tells the story of the nāga that, according to some locals, still lives in the lake. Markers are placed around a section of the lake to denote where boats are not allowed to go. These markers are said to show the place where the nāga resides.

CHAPTER 6

DRAGONS
of European
Cultural Myth

he dragons imagined by the peoples of Europe were very different from the serpents of Asian mythology. Although many of the European draconic tales, such as the Norse myths, date to before the Christian era, under the Church's influence they tended to evolve into morality tales. Dragons in European myth are rarely helpful to mankind, nor are they even neutral. They are almost always greedy, fire-breathing bullies who deserve nothing less than death at the hands of a worthy hero.

Perhaps because of this, a lot of the European dragon tales focus more on the humans who kill the dragons than on the beasts themselves. A whole host of heroes have assumed this role. Some are kings and noblemen, but, interestingly enough, a few of them are humble youths. As in many morality tales, such dragon stories often feature a worthy young man who, by accomplishing a dangerous and difficult task, finds himself rewarded with riches, a title, and possibly even a royal princess for his bride.

"The Powers whose name and shape
no living creature knows
Have pulled the Immortal Rose;
And though the Seven Lights bowed
in their dance and wept,
The Polar Dragon slept,
His heavy rings uncoiled from glimmering deep to deep:
When will he wake from sleep?"

—WILLIAM BUTLER YEATS, "AEDH PLEADS WITH THE
ELEMENTAL POWERS"

Dragons of Norse Myth and Scandinavia

The mythology of the Scandinavian people, created by the ancestral populations of Denmark, Norway, and Sweden, remain popular tales. The powerful king of the gods, Odin, together with his fellow deities such as Thor, the god of thunder, and Loki, the mischievous troublemaker, continue to serve as inspiration for everything from novels to movies to comic books. Not surprisingly, Norse mythology includes several tales in which dragons feature prominently.

The Midgard Serpent

This creature, named Jormungand, was so long that he could encircle the earth, holding his tail in his mouth while he did so. The Midgard Serpent was the son of the god Loki and the giantess Angerboda. He was expelled from the immortal realm by Odin and was forced to live under the sea holding his tail in his jaws so that he could not move from his imprisoned state.

The god of thunder, Thor, became the mortal foe of the Midgard Serpent—perhaps because the serpent was once party to a trick played upon the hot-tempered god. Jormungand changed his huge, serpentine body into the shape of a cat, and a giant king challenged Thor to prove his strength by lifting the creature off of the floor. The cat was not especially huge, but it weighed as much as the massive serpent that was its true form, and Thor was only able to lift it far enough so that one paw came off the floor. Although the giant king praised Thor's accomplishment—for even lifting a portion of the beast required a prodigious display of strength—the god did not forgive or forget.

One day, Thor wanted to go fishing with the giant Hymir. The giant refused to provide the bait for the fishing trip, so Thor used his mighty hammer to knock the head off of the giant's favorite ox. Using the severed head as bait for their massive hook, they rowed into the sea far enough to catch a couple of whales. This was not enough of a take for the thunder god, however, and despite Hymir's objections Thor rowed them farther out to sea and cast the ox head and its hook into very deep water.

They felt a tug on the line strong enough to nearly capsize the boat, but Thor pulled up his hook and found that the massive dragon had taken his bait. The Midgard Serpent glared balefully at the god, his jaws dripping with venom and blood. The serpent hissed and spread those massive jaws, whipping his head around as he tried to dislodge the hook. Hymir flew into a panic while Thor snatched up his hammer and prepared to crush the dragon's huge skull. Before he could deliver the blow, however, Hymir cut the line and Jormungand slipped back under the waves.

TWILIGHT OF THE GODS: THOR AND THE SERPENT'S LAST BATTLE

It was prophesized that Thor and the Midgard Dragon would face each other one more time, on the Day of the Last Battle—that is, when the world of the gods was destined to end, so that it could be reborn as a human realm. At that time a mighty war would break out, with gods, giants, demons, and monsters all fighting for survival. The tale of the great final battle is recounted as the climax of the Norse mythological canon.

When the fight erupted, Jormungand let go of his tail and slithered ashore, where he met the thunder god in the final battle. The dragon lashed and snapped at Thor, who evaded the attack and flung thunderbolts at the serpent to hold him at bay.

Finally, the god of thunder raised his great hammer and smashed it down on the serpent's head, crushing his skull and killing him. Thor raised his fist in triumph and began to stride away from the scene of his victory when a last exhalation of venomous breath rose from the dragon's bleeding, broken body. Thor breathed in his poison and he too fell dead beside the corpse of his greatest foe.

The Dragon Fafnir

In another tale that comes to us from the rich mythology of the Norsemen, Fafnir dwelt in a cave atop a pile of fabulous treasure. Among those treasures was a powerful ring, forged by Loki himself, worth an immeasurable amount of money—but also cursed its owner with eternal misfortune. Fafnir had been born a mighty dwarf, but he killed his father and ran away with the treasures—including the ring. He clutched his precious possessions to his chest and fled in a thrill of panic, delighted that he had stolen so many treasures but desperately fearful that someone would come and take them away from him.

Hiding in a mountain cave at last, he laid the treasures in a great pile and threw his body on top of them. There he lay for a very long time, and over the years his greed and selfishness corrupted him into a poisonous beast, capable only of guarding his hoard and slaying any mortal foolish enough to come after it. His body became long and reptilian, covered with scales and sprouting giant, leathery wings. Poison coursed through his veins and polluted his breath. Thus did the dwarf Fafnir become the dragon Fafnir.

That treasure was coveted by many, including the dwarf Regin, who was Fafnir's brother. Regin knew the worth of the valuable hoard, but he also feared the power of the dragon. He needed to find a mortal agent to kill the wyrm. He found this instrument in Prince Sigurd, a young man whose family had been favored by Odin with a magic sword. Sigurd's father had been slain and the sword shattered into three pieces. Regin approached Sigurd with a plan: He would help the prince restore the sword, and then lead him to a fabulous treasure. Sigurd would wield his mighty sword, and they would both become very rich from the dragon's treasure.

Together the man and the dwarf reforged the sword. The dwarf was a master smith, but in the end it was Sigurd's own skill, and the legacy of his father's blood, that reforged the blade. After many previous attempts had resulted in the blade breaking again, they at last succeeded in reforging the sword. Sigurd took the weapon he had recreated and used it to slice the anvil into two parts. The weapon was at last ready for the great quest.

To the Dragon's Lair

Regin led Sigurd to the cave where Fafnir lurked. The young prince trembled in fear when he saw the huge footprints left by the beast in the mud of a riverbank, where the dragon came to drink each morning. The treacherous Regin outlined a plan: Sigurd should dig a deep hole in the ground beside that path, hiding there with the mighty sword until Fafnir passed on his way to the water. When the beast's soft underbelly was exposed, Sigurd would stab upward, killing the wyrm.

The dwarf withdrew to a safe distance as Sigurd set to digging. As his pit grew deeper, an old man approached. He watched, approvingly, obviously understanding the prince's purpose. Finally he spoke up, and suggested that Sigurd dig a shallow pit to the side of the first one, a small shelter just large and deep enough to hold a man.

"The dragon's blood will kill you, otherwise," the old man explained. "And you should know that the dwarf Regin knows this fact very well. It would seem that he wants you to die so he can claim the treasure for himself."

Sigurd rightly perceived that the old man was none other than Odin, king of the gods. No fool, the mortal followed the god's suggestion and excavated a small pit beside the deep one that would catch the dragon's poisonous blood. As dawn's mist filtered through the forest, Sigurd felt the ground vibrate underneath his feet, thrumming from the dragon's mighty footsteps. The prince crouched in his pit and held his breath as the dragon, stinking of vile poison, lumbered past. When the creature's belly was over his head, Sigurd thrust his blade deep, then quickly rolled into his shallow pit.

The dragon roared and flailed, thrashing his tail and snapping with his fanged jaws, but he could not reach the human tormentor. As his blood drained away, the dragon's struggles slowly eased until, finally, he died. The streaming blood filled the deep pit Sigurd had excavated, but he stayed dry in the other one he had created on the advice of the stranger.

Regin emerged from hiding, dashing toward the dragon's cave to claim the entire treasure for himself—only to discover, much to his surprise, that Sigurd still lived. The quick-thinking and treacherous dwarf suggested that Sigurd should cook the dragon's heart, and that Regin would then devour the morsel as a tribute to the young prince's heroism.

Justice Served

Sigurd, still not entirely sure what to make of the dwarf, agreed. But he vowed to himself that he would remain cautious and alert. He sliced the heart out of the dragon's corpse and began to cook it over a hot fire. When he turned the heart to char it evenly, he burned his fingers on some of the juice, as the dragon's blood came sizzling out. Without thinking, he licked his fingers and was astounded at the magical effect of the blood: He could understand the language of the birds as they chattered in the trees around him.

The birds gave the prince counsel, informing him that if he ate the heart himself he would gain immortal wisdom. Upon consuming the gruesome repast, Sigurd perceived that Regin intended to kill him, so that the dwarf could keep the treasure for himself. Thus forewarned, Sigurd turned the tables on the villainous Regin, slaying him and claiming the treasure. This, of course, would lead to an assortment of further adventures, all because the hero with a great sword slew the dragon Fafnir.

THE EVOLUTION OF
FAFNIR'S STORY

This tale, first told as a story of Norse mythology, became the foundation for many other stories. Sigurd, renamed Siegfried, became a central figure in Germanic myth, including Richard Wagner's masterwork, *The Ring of the Nibelung*, in which the Christian ethos is mixed with the theme of revenge. Other elements, including the broken sword remade, and the power of a magic ring, became central features of J. R. R. Tolkien's masterpiece, *The Lord of the Rings*.

Beowulf and the Fire Dragon

Beowulf the King had ruled Geatland, a kingdom in the southern part of Sweden, for fifty peaceful and prosperous years. As a young man, the monarch had made a great name for himself when he had sailed to Denmark to do battle with a savage monster named Grendel that for twelve years had been ravaging the kingdom of King Hrothgar. Beowulf slew Grendel and then followed up his accomplishment by killing the monster's equally fearsome mother who had come seeking revenge. The rewards, both material and in reputation, for his exploit had elevated him to the throne of his own realm when he returned to Sweden. Beowulf spent most of his years in peace, ruling the Geats.

But Beowulf was confronted with one last challenge, a creature he must face that was even more horrible than those he had slain in his youth. The beast was roused because of the foolishness of one of the king's own servants, who had run away from the king's steading to avoid punishment for some minor infraction. The runaway servant came upon a vast barrow mound, an ancient burial site, on a cliff near the sea.

Seeking shelter, the servant crept inside the vast, hollow holding, which turned out to be the burial site of a long-forgotten nobleman. Advancing cautiously into the darkness, the servant was startled to realize that a dim source of illumination brightened the chamber in front of him. As he moved closer, he was first surprised and delighted to observe a large mound of treasures: gold and silver heaped high in the form of coins, swords, bejeweled armor and helmets, and other amazing objects. Clearly this was the burial hall of a great but forgotten king. Only then did the young man discern the source of the illumination: It was the glowing fire emitted from the nostrils of a huge, sleeping dragon.

Still, the servant could not pass up this opportunity. Suspecting that if he brought a valuable treasure back to the king he could deflect the punishment that otherwise would be his fate, he stealthily picked up a single golden goblet. Retracing his steps carefully, he silently left the barrow and broke into a run, carrying the treasure back with him.

The Serpent Aroused

However, this dragon had that keen and greedy eye for its possessions that is a trait of the species. As soon as it awakened, it noticed that one of its treasures had been stolen, and its rage knew no bounds. Though it had been secure in the barrow for 300 years, the monster immediately emerged and flew the length and breadth of Geatland, laying waste to the farms and towns of the humans wherever it found them.

Beowulf knew he would have to fight this monster, but he despairingly felt the weight of his years. He understood his duty, but for him this was not the epic adventure he had embraced in his younger years. Instead, bowed under a burden of fatalistic responsibility and sadness, he embarked upon this new, and final, quest.

He prepared himself carefully, donning a suit of mail armor, placing an iron helm with face and cheek guards on his head, and strapping to his belt a sturdy, reliable sword. Instead of his usual shield of linden wood, he ordered his smith to make him a shield of iron, in the hope that this would stand up to the fiery heat of the dragon's breath. Thus armed, he set forth, accompanied by a small band of his loyal supporters. The runaway servant whose theft had been the start of all the trouble was compelled to lead his king to the barrow where the dragon made his lair.

HOBBITRY

Fans of J. R. R. Tolkien's *The Hobbit* will have no difficulty, of course, in recognizing in this story the roots of Tolkien's prelude to *The Lord of the Rings*. Bilbo steals a single golden cup from the hoard of the mighty dragon Smaug. The dragon, upon awakening, misses the cup and comes forth from the Lonely Mountain bringing fire and terror.

Beowulf's Last Battle

Perhaps sensing—and disappointed by—the reluctance of his men to do battle with such a terrible foe, Beowulf stated that he would approach the barrow and fight the monster by himself. Only one man, Wiglaf—the youngest member of the party and the king's kinsman—asked to accompany Beowulf, but the elder hero denied the request. Instead, he approached the opening to the ancient burial mound by himself and called out a challenge to the monster within.

With a great blast of fire, the dragon emerged and immediately attacked. The billowing cloud of flame was partially deflected by the king's metal shield, but even so his hair was singed and his face blistered by the infernal heat. He struck upward with his sword, but the blade merely scraped along the monster's tough, almost impenetrable skin. Again the dragon breathed its fiery breath, and still the mighty hero stood up to the unspeakable punishment.

Behind Beowulf, his retainers cried out in terror at the horrible scene, turned, and fled for the imagined shelter of the nearby woods. Only Wiglaf held firm to his courage and his wits. Clutching his own sword, the young nobleman advanced to the aid of his king, as Beowulf struck again and again at the dragon's neck and head. One of these blows struck bone, and that caused the blade to shatter in his hand, disarming the king at a crucial moment.

Before Beowulf could draw his dagger, the dragon's head slashed down, knocking his shield out of the way. One of the creature's sharp fangs penetrated Beowulf's neck, drawing blood—and, more important, injecting lethal poison into the great hero's body. As the wounded king staggered back, the dragon struck again.

But this time Wiglaf was there, crouching beside his king. He saw a fleshy opening in the scales beneath the dragon's maw, and the young man thrust upward with his sword, penetrating the jaws and driving the dragon back. It breathed at them again, but now the heat of its infernal breath had been weakened.

Beowulf drew his dagger and Wiglaf raised his sword. Together the two men advanced and attacked the dragon, hacking at it again and again, finding more gaps in the scales, driving their metal blades deep into its foul flesh. Finally the serpent collapsed and breathed its last, lying dead in an expanding pool of blood. The king, succumbing to the poison at last, staggered and fell beside the monster.

In despair, Wiglaf brought forth a great armload of the treasure and laid it beside his king, but there would be no saving the old man. In his last breath, Beowulf declared that the vast wealth should be buried and not shared with the faithless people who had so cravenly deserted him. Surrounded by that treasure, and in view of his shamefaced retainers—who, now that the threat was gone, emerged from shelter to offer hollow comfort to their great monarch—the King of Geatland died.

He would be buried in a barrow of his own, on a great cliff above the sea. Wiglaf inherited his crown, and the epic tale of Beowulf's heroism and greatness would become a legend told among the peoples of Europe for many centuries to come.

"So comes snow after fire, and even dragons have their ending."

—J. R. R. TOLKIEN

AN EPIC OF OLD ENGLISH

Although the epic of Beowulf is the story of a hero from a Swedish realm who made his initial reputation by an achievement in Denmark, the tale has come to us as one of the earliest works of literature written in the English language. As a long-lived oral narrative, the story likely represents the contributions of many tellers. Certainly it had been told around hearths, campfires, and thrones for some centuries before it was first written down by monks around the year 1000.

Nidhogg and the World Tree

A central facet of Norse mythology, and indeed an aspect of many myths from around the world, is the idea of a mighty tree that either bears the world or stands at its center. The Norse called this tree Yggdrasil, and it was portrayed as a massive ash tree rising so high that its branches reached the heavens. It was supported by three roots, each of which extended to a different sacred well. The tree was very holy, and it supported many living creatures on the vast landscape of its branches.

The World Tree suffered many insults because of the animals living on it, but the most dangerous of these was caused by the serpent Nidhogg, which gnawed at one of its three roots from below. Some stories claimed that the roots prevented the dragon from emerging into the world; all the tales described the antics of a lively squirrel that ran up and down the tree, carrying messages from the serpent that lived under the tree to a mighty eagle that lived at its very top.

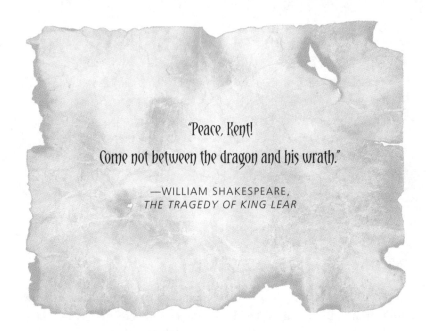

"Peace, Kent!
Come not between the dragon and his wrath."

—WILLIAM SHAKESPEARE,
THE TRAGEDY OF KING LEAR

Dragons of Olde England

Dragons hold a special place in British lore. The father of King Arthur was Uther Pendragon, and the symbol of the dragon was emblazoned on the banner of many English kings. King Harold Godwinson, who perished at the battle of Hastings, is shown with a white dragon banner on the famed Bayeux Tapestry, which gave a graphic portrayal of William of Normandy's invasion and conquest of England in 1066.

White dragons and red dragons have symbolized the enmity between England and Wales, respectively, for many centuries. The Anglo-Saxon kingdom of Wessex was long symbolized by a golden dragon.

Far more than heraldry, however, the images and stories of dragons have filled British culture in literature and children's fables. The small island country has given the world some of the most memorable of the dragon tales still remembered today.

The Wyvern of Mordiford

A young girl named Maud, from the village of Mordiford in Herefordshire, in the southwest part of England, very much wanted to have a pet of her own, but her parents—especially her stern father—would not allow her to have a dog or a cat. Instead, the girl would go into the surrounding forests, where she fed and cared for the wild animals, and they befriended her. On one of these excursions, she was delighted to find a small, winged creature tottering around on two legs, sniffing at a patch of flowers. The creature was shy and fluttered away when Maud approached.

However, the clever girl came back with a saucer of milk and was soon able to lure the little creature into her lap, where it greedily lapped up the milk. Delighted and excited by her find, she carried the creature home and proudly showed her parents her new pet. Both of them were appalled, for they recognized the creature as a baby wyvern—a two-legged version of the terrible dragons of legend. They bade Maud to take the animal back to where she found it and release it.

But the girl was willful as well as clever, and instead of releasing the baby wyvern she made a cage for it in a secret glade in the forest. Every day she returned with more milk, and as the wyvern drank the milk it grew quickly, and its natural draconic nature began to assert itself. Soon milk wasn't enough to sate it, and it broke free from its cage and flew deeper into the woods.

A Growing Menace

For a short time it survived on small forest animals that it caught, but it continued to grow, and so did its appetite. It killed and ate a sheep, and then another, and then it killed and devoured a cow. The farmer who owned the cow saw what had happened, and the villagers of Mordiford took up their sickles and pitchforks and went into the forest to try and kill the wyvern.

But the beast was too fast and too clever. While the men were hunting for it, the wyvern flew over their heads and attacked the village, killing and eating a chubby lad. Maud saw and recognized the creature, and when she approached it became gentle and affectionate, refusing to harm her. But she could not tame it, and when the angry villagers approached it flew away.

Now that the beast had tasted humans, it decided that men and women were its preferred meal, and it attacked again and again, killing and feeding on the villagers of Mordiford. In despair, they sought help from nearby nobles. One man, named Garston, came forward and offered to kill the creature. (In some versions of the story, Garston was a condemned prisoner who was promised his freedom if he could prevail; in others, he was a member of a noble family who offered to do the deed out of a sense of courage and honor.)

Garston prepared a trap. He took a large, sturdy barrel and studded the outside with a series of blades and hooks. Dragging the barrel into the path the wyvern was known to take, and then arming himself with a pistol, Garston climbed inside the barrel and watched through a single peephole to see what would happen.

The wyvern approached and smelled the delicious human flesh inside of the barrel. It bit at the stout wood, but could not crack it. Then the wyvern coiled itself around the barrel and tried to crush it with a great constriction of its serpentine body. But instead of breaking the barrel, the beast only succeeded in wounding itself, inflicting bloody cuts and slices all over its body. When the beast was exhausted and weakened, Garston fired his pistol through the peephole, and the impact of the bullet knocked the beast down.

Finally Garston burst from his barrel and used his knife to cut off the monster's head.

Maud, watching from nearby, wailed and cried over the death of her beloved pet, but the wyvern was finished—though not without a last gasp of revenge in at least one version of this story. That account claims that when Garston cut the head from the wyvern's serpentine neck, a last burst of poisonous gas escaped from the monster's lungs, and breathing these lethal fumes the wyvern-slayer was overcome, and died.

The Lambton Worm

At Fatfield, in County Durham in England, there are locations still known as Worm Well and Worm Hill, which trace their naming and lineage to a vile, legless dragon. Other versions of the story put the setting at Penshaw Hill, where stands a monument to this cautionary tale.

Every version of the story agrees that there was a lazy young nobleman, John Lambton, who rebelled against the strictures of society and his elders. Symbolic of his wastrel ways, Lambton went fishing on a Sunday when he should have been at church. An old man came by and warned him that his irresponsibility could lead only to a bad outcome. But John Lambton laughed off the warning and continued to fish—though he caught nothing until the church bells rang to signal the end of the service.

At this point Lambton hooked a small eel or snake—some versions say that it had short legs and was several feet long, while others place it only as the size of a man's thumb. Disgusted by his catch, the young fisherman turned for home, only to once again meet the old man. This time the elder suggested that Lambton had hooked the devil himself.

Laughing off the notion, John threw the worm down a local well and went about his business. According to the story he grew up to be a moral and chivalrous man and, in order to atone for his earlier wastrel ways, went off to the Holy Land as a participant in one of the Crusades. He would be gone from home for seven long years. While he was away, circumstances at Lambton took a serious turn. The water from the well in which—unbeknownst to his neighbors—young Lambton had thrown the worm became poisonous and, though it was conveniently located and for centuries had been a reliable source of good water, the site had to be abandoned. Not long afterward, livestock started to disappear from local farms, and rumors of a dangerous beast swept through the area.

To their horror, the people of Lambton discovered a great, snakelike serpent living in the Wear River, emerging at night to feed. They realized that the monster came from the now-ruined well, and it had become so huge that it could coil at least seven times around a nearby hill. It ate cows and sheep and was blamed for the disappearance of several small children. Several villagers went forth in an attempt to slay the worm, but it killed all of its attackers. A couple of the swordsmen managed to hack pieces of the serpent's flesh away, but after slaughtering the men the worm slithered over to the bloody pieces and reattached them to its great body.

Finally, the worm crossed the Wear River and crept toward Lambton Hall, the ancestral manor that was the hall of the family, and the place where John's father, now an old man, still ruled as lord. Acting on the advice of his chief servant, the lord ordered that a large trough be filled with the fresh milk of nine cows, some twenty gallons worth. The serpent smelled the milk as it approached, and drank the trough empty. Thus sated, it returned to its hill and slept.

A visiting knight came past the realm and heard the story. He attempted to slay the wyrm, attacking with his lance, but the monster used its great tail to uproot trees, using the heavy trunks as cudgels so that it could beat the knight to death. The beast returned to Lambton Hall every day, and if the trough was not completely filled it would uproot a nearby tree and use it to smash and destroy. Sometimes it would sleep coiled around its hill, while at other times it went back into the river and wrapped itself around a great rock.

This went on for several years, and finally John Lambton returned from the Crusade to find his father in despair and the Lambton estate virtually destitute because of the depredations of the greedy wyrm. Again, John met the old man he had seen while he was fishing. The old man reminded John of his warning. Stricken by grief and a sense of responsibility, John suspected that the wyrm was the eel he had caught as a young man. He knew that he must do something to get rid of it.

Having heard the tales of the others who fought and died against the beast, he sought out the advice of an old, wise woman, rumored to be a witch. Whether or not that was true, she gave him good advice, telling him to plant spearheads all around his armor, pointing outward. She warned him, however, that if he was successful in killing the serpent, he would also have to kill the next living creature he saw after the beast was dead. If he failed to do this, a curse would fall over his family for the next nine generations.

Lambton prepared his armor as the old woman had described. He told his father that he would blow his hunting horn three times if he was successful; upon hearing the horn, the lord was to release

John's hound, which would run to its master. Thus, instead of killing a person, John could slay the dog in order to avoid the curse that the old woman had foretold. When John was ready, he sought the wyrm at the bank of the river and goaded it into attacking him. The beast wrapped itself around the man in his blade-studded armor and tried to squeeze him to death. The harder it squeezed, however, the more the spearheads dug into its flesh. As pieces of the serpent were cut away, they fell into the river and were carried away by the current, so the monster could not patch itself back together. Finally, the bloody wyrm died, and Lambton cut off its head.

He blew the horn as planned, but his father, in his delight at the news, forgot the cautionary tale and ran to the riverside. He was the first living creature the victorious warrior saw, but he could not bring himself to commit patricide. Instead, the hound that arrived moments later was killed. But that was not enough to ward off the curse, and history records that the Lambton men were felled by tragic causes for many generations to come.

THE KNUCKER

A knucker is a water dragon that lived in murky fresh water bogs, ponds, and cesspools in southern England. For this reason, such bodies of water were sometimes referred to as "knuckerholes." Knuckerholes were first observed in the area of Sussex, and were reputedly bottomless. The water in them did not freeze, no matter how cold the weather got during winter. Although knuckers had small wings, they were not necessarily capable of flight—the wings in fact served more like the fins on a fish. Knuckers moved exceptionally well through the water. They did not, though, have gills and needed to breathe air. Like crocodiles and alligators, their eyes and nostrils were atop a broad, flat head. This allowed a knucker to observe its surroundings while keeping the bulk of itself underwater.

Knuckers had large heads and huge mouths, while the body was long and serpentine, as sinuous as that of an eel's. They did not have legs but moved snakelike across the ground and could use their tail to strike down animals they wished to eat. They were fast enough to pursue their prey this way, catching cows, sheep, and humans; supposedly a horse could out-run a pursuing knucker. Their bite was exceptionally venomous, and some reports claimed that the poison was so acidic that it actually dissolved the flesh of the victim.

The Knuckerslayer

The most famous knucker terrorized the area of Lyminster, in West Sussex. It grew to a massive length and emerged nightly from its hole, feasting on the farm animals it hunted for miles around, and sometimes killing and eating travelers it encountered on the roads. Folk learned to stay off those roads after dark, and farmers took to locking their sheep and cattle up in barns at sunset.

But even that didn't solve the problem, as the knucker, increasingly hun-gry, began to batter down walls and destroy buildings to get at the meat it could smell inside. Its moaning roar and sinister hiss were audible for miles. The mayor of Lyminster offered a significant reward for anyone who could kill the knucker, and the king of Sussex was said to offer his daughter's hand in marriage to the nobleman who could bring proof of the knucker's death. Several knights took up these offers. Each arrived in the area, determined to best the monster. One by one they rode forth to do battle, but none of them was ever heard from again.

Finally a young man named Jim, who came from a village near Lyminster, approached the mayor with a plan. He explained that he needed the assistance of the people of the city, and in particular the bakers; the mayor eagerly ordered the citizens to help. Under Jim's instructions, the folk assembled the ingredients to bake a huge pie. Local alchemists contributed a variety of poisons, and Jim made sure that all of these toxins were included in the recipe.

When it was finally ready, the mayor provided a large cart and a draft horse to Jim. The pie was loaded into the cart and Jim, by himself, led the horse and its load out to the knuckerhole. He intended to leave the pie and retreat with the horse and the cart, but he was unable to unload the heavy pie before the sun set and the water in the knuckerhole boiled upward with movement.

Jim hastily retreated into the nearby woods, taking only his axe with him. The horse panicked as the knucker emerged, but it was still lashed to the cart and so couldn't escape. The knucker's jaws spread wide, and it gulped down the terrified animal in a couple of gory bites. Then it turned its attention to the pie, which was still warm enough that the sumptuous odors of onions, cheese, and mincemeat wafted up from the huge dish. With another gulp the knucker swallowed the pie, and the cart as well, chewing noisily as it splintered the wood planks of the two-wheeled vehicle.

Made sluggish by the meal, and perhaps already under the influence of the poison, the knucker slid along one of its paths through the woods. Jim, clutching his axe, followed. After less than a mile the knucker came to a stop, thrashing and moaning as the poisons wracked its body. It took nearly until dawn before the fearsome creature died, but when it had expired Jim approached it and chopped off its great head with the axe.

With tremendous effort, Jim dragged the head back to town, where he was hailed as a hero and received the mayor's reward—enough for him to buy his own house and live in style for the rest of his life. (Not being a nobleman, however, he was not granted the hand of the princess in marriage.) When he finally died, his cleverness and heroism were still remembered, and he was interred in Saint Mary Magdalene's Church, underneath an impressive gravestone that, to this day, is called the Slayer's Slab.

THE DRAGONS OF LINDESFARNE ABBEY

The Isle of Lindesfarne was a sanctified bit of land off the east coast of northern England. It was home to a colony of monks who worked hard copying down holy books. The monks also recorded the daily events of their lives, and these accounts included reports of dragons flying through the skies, thrashing the monastery with lightning, terrorizing the monks with their supernatural power.

In 793 the monastery was attacked and destroyed, and the monks were slain and their treasures taken. At first, it was assumed that dragons had sacked the place, but a few survivors emerged from the rubble to report that longships, their prows bearing the carved heads of fierce dragons, had come across the North Sea. They had pulled onto the beaches of the island, and fierce, bloodthirsty Viking raiders had come ashore to pillage the place.

In Lindesfarne, the rumors of actual dragons proved to be false, though the death and devastation were all too real. The attack on Lindesfarne is generally regarded as the first raid carried out by the Vikings, a people that would plague the continent of Europe, and even the coast of North Africa, for the next few centuries. The ships of those Vikings, wherever they were seen, were called "dragonships."

Childe Wynde and the Dragon

The King of Northumberland had two grown children: a son named Childe Wynde and a daughter named Margaret. Childe Wynde was a bold knight and a great leader of men, while Margaret was a maid of kindness, grace, and no little beauty. Their mother, the queen, had died while the children were young, but the king lived happily into his old age. His daughter kept the king company while Childe Wynde and his company of soldiers sailed from England to wage war in a distant land.

Margaret and the rest of the king's subjects were surprised one day when the monarch announced that he would remarry. No one knew how the king had made the arrangements to take a new wife, but she soon arrived at Bamburgh Castle, the king's palace, by ship. The people made her welcome, and the princess greeted her graciously, but all were left with the feeling that the new queen was cold and aloof. Rumors quickly spread through the castle, the servants whispering that she had a deep cruel streak and would beat those whose service she found wanting.

But the king was happy, and when the day of the wedding arrived he took the lady as his second wife and hosted a grand celebration with feasting and drinking lasting all through the night. Only the queen remained aloof from the festivities. That night, while her new husband lay in drunken sleep, she sat up alone in the moonlight and wove a tapestry with silver thread. She worked the thread into many intricate symbols, all of them surrounding the image of a sleeping princess.

A Princess Transformed

It was near dawn when Margaret awakened in agony. Her limbs felt leaden, as if they were burdened down with great stones. She tried to raise her hand and cried out in terror as a wicked, taloned paw reached for her face. Tumbling out of bed, she tore the quilt to pieces and found herself unable to stand. A great tail lashed about the chamber, smashing the bed, knocking the curtains from the windows, bashing the wardrobe to pieces. Margaret tried to avoid the tail, crawling across the flagstone floor, but gradually—and much to her horror—she realized it was her own!

She lurched to the remnant of the shattered mirror and screamed at the image of her reflection: a scaly green face with twisted horns, a huge mouth, and fang-studded jaws. Her scream emerged as a bestial roar, and she recoiled backward at the realization that she had become a dragon.

Cries of alarm rang through the castle, and she heard the clanking footsteps of armored men charging toward her door. In horror and panic she went to the window and pushed her great body through the tight opening. Though she was high up in a tower, she leaped, and instinctively her great wings bore the weight of her new body, carrying her in a long glide past the castle wall. She was only vaguely aware of guards and courtiers shouting and pointing, and she didn't even feel the arrows of a few archers that struck her scaled skin only to bounce harmlessly away.

Coming to rest on the ground, Margaret felt a new sensation. Her nostrils picked up a sweet, alluring smell that she only vaguely recognized as being sheep; and then her stomach uttered a savage growl. She was terribly hungry—starving practically—and with a great leap she took to the air again, gliding over the houses of the village and landing in the midst of a flock of sheep. She was barely aware of her actions as she killed the helpless creatures, gulping down one after the other until her hunger was finally sated.

Only then did horror set in as she realized what she had done. Once again she took to the air, this time flying to the crest of a nearby mountain. She curled among the sharp, bare rocks there, laid her head on her forepaws, and collapsed in despair.

Horror and Dismay

The people, too, despaired, fearing that a dragon had come to devour the princess and terrorize the land. The new queen declared this was the case, and the citizenry, and even the court nobles, muttered among themselves that it was a shocking bit of evil to know that the dragon had arrived on the very night the queen had wed their steadfast king.

One old man, however, perceived the truth. He went to the king privately and told him that dark magic had transformed his daughter into the dragon. The only solution he could suggest was to urge the king to recall his son, Childe Wynde, from the war and bring him home to deal with the crisis in the realm. He also urged the king to cast out or destroy his new wife, but this the king would not do. Instead, the queen would remain secure in her own tower, protected by stout locks from the vengeance of the aroused populace.

In due time, Childe Wynde received the message from his father. Appalled at the magic that had afflicted his sister, he delayed only long enough to construct a ship from the wood of pear trees, since that timber was well known to be proof against sorcery. Then the prince and his company sailed for Northumberland.

A Hero's Homecoming

Childe Wynde sailed within sight of Bamburgh Castle, which stood high on a headland above the seashore. Before he could enter the harbor, however, a swarm of sea furies, enchanted creatures that delighted in the destruction of sailors and their ships, arose around his vessel. The sea churned in a great storm, and a whirlpool threatened to suck it into the depths. But the pear wood was strong, and though the sea furies hurled themselves against the hull, the timbers held and the ship made it safely into the harbor.

The queen, who had summoned the furies with her spells, watched in rage from her high tower as the prince's crew dropped anchor. She had one more trick in her vile arsenal, however: Pulling out some of the threads from her tapestry, she took command of Margaret's draconic form like a puppet master might operate his marionette. With a single bark of command, she sent the dragon into the air, demanding that it destroy the ship and kill all the men who were coming ashore.

The dragon flew low over the shore and spat a great cloud of fire at the ship, causing it to burst into flames. The prince and his crew hurled themselves into the shallow water and waded ashore as the burning ship settled and threw up a great cloud of steam, obscuring the air over the water and the beach.

Childe Wynde dragged himself on land. He couldn't see through the mist, until he spotted a gleaming yellow circle—not the sun, but the dragon's eye. He drew his sword, fearing that his sister, bewitched by sorcery, was about to attack him. Indeed, the dragon's mouth gaped wide—but instead of biting, he heard words in his sister's voice. In a desperate act of love, her own will had triumphed over the sorcery just enough for her to whisper to her brother.

She told him that he must kiss her three times upon the mouth, even though her scaly flesh would slash and wound him. Then he was to take a piece of wood from the hull of his ship and seek out the queen, his stepmother.

Childe Wynde stepped into the dragon's embrace and kissed her. Sharp spines lined the scales around her mouth, and these tore at his skin, causing his lips to bleed. But he pressed forward and kissed her again, even though still more blood flowed from even deeper cuts. Ignoring the pain, he kissed her a third time, though one of the spines speared right through his cheek.

When he stepped back, the dragon sank to the ground, shriveled and dead. Within its vast sack of skin a small figure moved, and when the men cut through they found the princess Margaret, pale and shaken but as beautiful as ever. The prince wasted no time in taking for a cudgel one of the charred beams of his ship's hull. With his sister and soldiers following, he marched up to the castle and confronted his father.

The king was overjoyed to have his daughter back, but so powerful was the thrall that held him that he would not consent to allow his new wife to be punished. But Childe Wynde made a reasonable request. He asked to merely touch her with the piece of pear wood. If she was not a witch, the wood would do her no harm.

To this, the king agreed, and when the two men entered the queen's chambers they found her cowering behind a tapestry. She shrieked in terror when Childe Wynde raised the pear wood cudgel, collapsing and changing into her true form. The king stared, aghast, as his wife was revealed to be a wart-covered, vile-smelling toad. Both the king and the prince stood back as the creature hopped out of the castle and away, where it would never be seen by humans again.

Dragons of French Legend

Dragons play an important role in the symbols, myths, and fairy tales of France. The Gallic druids in the pre-Christian era used to tattoo draconic images onto their skin. Because these druids were significant enemies to the Romans who eventually conquered Gaul (France), the dragon was a natural symbol of an enemy. But sometimes that enemy could be tamed by a pure (and perhaps Christian) heart.

"Though Philip the Second
Of France was reckoned
No coward, his breath came short
When they told him a dragon
As big as a wagon
Was waiting below in the court!
A dragon so long, and so wide, and so fat,
That he couldn't get in at the door to chat:
The king couldn't leave him
Outside and grieve him,
He had to receive him
Upon the mat,
The dragon bowed nicely,
And very concisely
He stated the reason he'd called:
He made the disclosure
With frigid composure.
King Philip was simply appalled!
He demanded for eating, a fortnight apart,
The monarch's ten daughters, all dear to his heart.
'And now you'll produce,' he
Concluded, 'the juicy
And succulent Lucie
By way of start!'"

—GUY WETMORE CARRYL, EXCERPT FROM "HOW THOMAS A
    MAID FROM A DRAGON RELEASED," 1902

The Tarasque

The Tarasque is a creature well known in the region of Provence, France. Indeed, the village of Tarascon is named for this mythical beast, which is described as being a mix of several formidable creatures. It was amphibious, dwelling in a forest much of the time, but perfectly capable of swimming. The Rhone River was a favorite hunting ground of the Tarasque, and it was known to sink boats and eat humans whenever it had the opportunity.

The Tarasque was really a nightmarish mix of animals. Described as a kind of dragon, it had the head of a lion, a sturdy body protected by a turtle's shell, with a lashing, scaly tail tipped with a venomous stinger, like a scorpion. It had six short, bear-like legs and was a vicious predator and famous menace to all the peoples of southern France.

It was said that the king of Nerluc organized his knights and even equipped them with catapults so that they could do battle with this beast. Despite their courage and skill, however, the Tarasque drove the human warriors away and inflicted heavy casualties.

As with so many of the famous and feared beasts of history, it took the hand of a gentle woman—in the person of Saint Martha, a famed miracle-worker—to at last defeat the Tarasque. She is said to have charmed the creature with her cross, by reciting hymns and prayers and by sprinkling it with holy water. Cowed and meek in the presence of such blessed goodness, the creature quietly followed her to a nearby village.

The villagers, of course, were appalled at the arrival of the beast, and they attacked and killed the creature, which made no effort to defend itself. After Martha preached to them and converted many of them to Christianity, they regretted their hasty violence and, in symbolic atonement, renamed their village Tarascon in honor of the beast they had slain.

The Dragon of Rhodes

This dragon did not lair in France, but it was slain by a Frenchman, Dieudonne de Gozon of Languedoc. The story occurred around 1340 and was recorded in contemporary sources, making it one of the most recent human/dragon encounters on record.

De Gozon was a member of the Knights of Rhodes, an order of Crusader Knights established on the important island in the Aegean Sea. The Crusades, originally intended to reclaim the Holy Land of Christendom, had mostly ended in failure by the mid 1300s, and the Christian knights had established several strong points along the border between their realms and the areas of Turkey, the Middle East, and North Africa, which were controlled by Islamic forces. One of these fortresses was the Island of Malta, near Sicily, and another was at Rhodes.

The primary mission of these knights was to hold their fortified island against Muslim attacks, which came frequently and with growing force. Every one of the knights on the island was sworn to serve the Grand Master of the Knights of Rhodes, and this lord ordered all of his men to focus on their defenses, improving the fortifications and making ready to repel the next attack.

However, a dragon dwelt in a swampy realm on the interior of the island, and the beast was making a nuisance of itself by killing livestock and even sometimes claiming the life of innocent pilgrims or travelers. Several knights pleaded for permission from the grand master to sally forth against the beast, but this permission was denied because such a quest was a distraction from the order's primary mission.

De Gozon, however, was convinced by the pleas of the island's citizenry that the dragon must be killed. He disobeyed orders, donning his armor, hoisting his lance, and riding forth to slay the beast. He met the dragon near the edge of its swamp. When the serpent attacked, de Gozon's horse panicked, bucked off the knight, and thundered away. Armed only with his lance and his sword, and on foot, the knight faced the charging dragon.

The creature exhaled a blast of fiery breath, scorching the knight's armor and forcing him backward. De Gozon swung his sword, but the dragon ducked out of the way. With a swipe of its great claw it knocked the blade from the knight's hand, leaving him only his heavy horseman's lance. The knight picked up the lance, anchored the butt on the ground, and raised the tip as the dragon charged again. As the monster opened its maw to spew another blast of fire, the knight lunged, driving the lance head through the roof of the dragon's mouth and into its wicked brain, killing it instantly.

Cutting the head off the dragon, de Gozon took his trophy back to the fortress and nailed it above one of the gates. Despite his victory, the grand master was enraged at this act of disobedience and ordered the knight to be stripped of his rank and imprisoned in the deepest dungeon on the island. He languished there for some time, until the pleas for justice on his behalf—coming from both the citizens and his fellow knights—persuaded the master to free him and restore him to his place in the order.

HISTORICAL FOOTNOTE

From then on de Gozon was known by the nickname *Extinctor Draconis* ("Dragon Slayer"). Within a few years the grand master died and in 1346 de Gozon was awarded that title himself. Two years later he led the knights on a bold campaign to defeat the army of the Sultan of Egypt in Armenia, and his reign as Grand Master of the Knights of Rhodes was a successful one. The trophy of the dragon's skull remained on the fortress gate for some five hundred years, and in the 1800s a scientist was able to identify it as that of a crocodile.

Slavic Dragons

From Poland to the Ukraine to Russia and
the Baltic States, the Slavic world has its
own versions of the mighty, destructive
serpent myth. Some of the legends date
to the prehistory of the area, while others
are given names of Turkish or Persian etymol-
ogy, probably inspired by or symbolic of the waves
of invaders that swept into Russia from Mongolia, the steppes of Asia, and
Turkey. The Christian-era story of St. George slaying the dragon of Silene is
well known in Russia, and the dragonslayer himself is depicted on the coat
of arms for the city of Moscow.

Gorynych

Gorynych, a figure of Russian legend, was one of the most horrific and fearsome dragons in all of European myth (he also features in Ukrainian folk
tales). The creature was said to have three heads, each of which was capped
with twin horns like a goat's, and could spit a cloud of lethal fire. At the other
end of the body, seven lashing tails were tipped with horny spikes capable of
inflicting lethal damage. Gorynych was always surrounded by the smell of
sulphur, the stench of which sometimes gave his intended victims enough
warning that they could try to hide or flee.

He walked upright on his powerful hind legs, with short forelegs con-
nected to membranous wings. The forelegs were tipped with claws made of
iron, hard and sharp enough to tear through a soldier's armor or rip apart
a stone wall. While Gorynych was not a true flyer, he could glide on those
wings if he leaped from a great height. Given enough space, he could run at
high speed, roaring horribly, and launch himself into the air high enough
to swoop down upon his intended victim.

Gorynych was said to be able, on occasion, to take a bite out of the moon or the sun, resulting in an eclipse. The Russians took heart from the fact that the loss of the cosmic orb always proved temporary, and some teachings of the Orthodox Church suggested that this was proof that good would always eventually triumph over evil.

Gorynych Takes a Captive Wife

The wicked dragon had an uncle, Nemal Chelovek, who was a powerful sorcerer and a very evil man. Chelovek intended to make the dragon the ruler of all Russia, and to this end he kidnapped the tsar's daughter and imprisoned her in his dark castle high in the Ural Mountains. The heartbroken tsar offered a tremendous reward for the hero who could rescue his daughter. Many bold warriors ventured into the mountains on the quest to save the princess and earn the treasure, but none were ever heard from again. Occasionally, the blood-spattered horse of one of the knights would come limping back down from the heights, suggesting the intrepid warrior's fate.

Chelovek was so secure in his mountain fastness that he did not have any guards in the place; the only occupants were the wizard, the dragon, and the captive princess. Still, the sorcerer was unafraid, and none of those knights who came up to rescue the princess had even been able to so much as find the castle.

Chelovek could turn himself into a giant and often did so, patrolling the valleys approaching his formidable castle. In this guise he crushed several of the knights who sallied there. Others were attacked on the mountain trails by Gorynych, sometimes killed by fire, sometimes by his powerful jaws, and otherwise by his iron talons or slashing tails.

An Unlikely Hero

A young palace guard in Moscow named Ivan was not known for any great fighting ability, but he had the unique capacity to understand the speech of birds. While on duty in the tsar's garden, the guard heard two crows talking about a secret castle in the Urals where a beautiful woman was being held prisoner. The crows had flown over the mountain crest, where a hidden trail snaked along, out of view of anyone in the castle or the surrounding valleys.

Deducing that this was the prison wherein the tsar's daughter was imprisoned, the guard approached the monarch and told him what he had heard. Though obviously afraid, he pledged that he would seek the secret path and try to reach the castle and rescue the princess. The tsar was so impressed by the young man's courage that he gave him a magic sword to aid him on his quest.

Traveling alone and on foot, Ivan went up into the mountains by a roundabout way and found the pathway along the crest. After many days of grueling travel, during which he was lashed by icy storms and terrified by crashing thunder and explosive lightning, he discovered the castle. Climbing down a steep slope, he entered the open gate. Once again he heard crows talking, and he knew where to find the chamber where the princess was chained.

However, the sorcerer sensed the presence of an intruder. In giant form he lumbered back to the castle, bellowing for Gorynych to come and join him in killing the human. Ivan, climbing the stairs to the high tower, heard the roar and turned to face the giant as Chelovek charged with an upraised club the size of a tree trunk. The sword flew from Ivan's hand unbidden and struck the giant in the heart, killing him and passing through his body. While the young soldier watched, helpless, the blade continued to fly through the air, spiraling down the long staircase. As the three-headed dragon came charging through the great hall, the sword slashed side to side, cutting each head from the neck and killing the dragon at once.

Ivan rescued the princess and returned to the tsar's palace. On the journey home the two fell in love, and after receiving his reward, Ivan, now an honored nobleman, was allowed to marry the princess.

Tugarin Zmeyevich

This dragon preyed on the people of the region around Kiev, capital of the Ukraine. He was a fire dragon with huge, but very flimsy, wings. Tugarin made himself a plague on the countryside, stealing livestock, burning buildings, and slaying all who tried to do him in.

He was pursued and eventually battled by a Ukrainian folk hero, Alyosha Popovich, who was the youngest of three brothers of an adventuring family. While his elder siblings were brawny fighters, Alyosha studied to be a priest and was known to rely on his wits and cunning more than his strength.

The duel between Alyosha and Tugarin is told in many versions among the eastern Slavic peoples. One of the most common has the two opponents finally meeting in a broad, open field. Tugarin hissed like a snake and used magic to send fiery attacks at the human. The dragon used his power over fire as he tried to choke the man with a thick cloud of smoke, assailed him with showers of sparks, and finally threw smoldering, charred logs at him. Alyosha avoided all these attacks but was unable to strike a blow against the dragon.

Finally, Tugarin took to the air, extending his broad wings—wings pale and thin as paper—and flew high above the field. There he soared in a circle, climbing ever higher, ready to swoop down on the adventurer and crush him.

But Tugarin, a creature of fire, was taken by surprise by a sudden rainstorm. He was drenched, and his wings shredded away like the paper they resembled. Helpless and terrified, the dragon plunged to the ground where he crashed, insensate.

Finally Alyosha Popovich was able to approach the dragon. He used his sword to cut the beast into pieces, scattered those chunks all across the field, and claimed the head as his prize.

SYMBOLIZING DANGER

Tugarin became a symbol to the Slavic people of the terrible dangers that beset the endless steppes of their land. Since his name was of Turkish derivation, it's also theorized that Tugarin symbolized the Mongols, who conquered much of central Asia at different points in its history.

Krak's Dragon

Krakow is a large city in southern Poland. It is located on the banks of the Vistula River and is not far from the Carpathian Mountains. A common legend declares that the city took its name because of the exploit of a clever young dragonslayer named Krak.

Before the city was founded, and some seven centuries before the start of the Christian era, the area was a region of villages and small towns all under the loose regency of a tribal king. An elevation called Wawel Hill rose along the bank of the Vistula River, and at its foot was a deep and dark cave. Its mouth lay almost even with the water level, and deep within its dark recesses lived a savage, fire-breathing dragon.

The dragon, like many of those hailing from Slavic realms, had two powerful rear legs and very small forelegs—the front legs were actually part of the wings, rather like those of a pterodactyl. It had a huge mouth, and its jaw could stretch wide enough to gulp down a whole sheep. It also had keen eyes that were able to see even in dim light, and a long tail that the dragon could use as a bone-crushing weapon.

The dragon had terrorized the region for many years. It killed livestock, especially sheep and pigs, and sometimes pounced upon unwary travelers. It had a fondness for shiny baubles, and though the region was not rich, over the decades the dragon managed to amass a decent hoard of treasure. This hoard included mainly coins, but also necklaces and rings of precious stones, ornaments used by priests and shamans, and so forth. As the dragon's reputation spread, brave fighters came to seek it and try to kill it. But men armed with spears and swords were no match for the dragon, which incinerated the would-be dragonslayers with a blast of fiery breath.

The district was ruled by a tribal king who was keenly conscious that the wealth of his realm was suffering badly due to the dragon's depredations. Rather than live in such a cursed location, people were picking up and leaving. By the time the king's beautiful daughter had come of age, he was at his wit's end. Lacking any other recourse, he pledged his daughter's hand in marriage to any man who proved his worth by slaying the dragon.

The offer, of course, drew an additional number of brave warriors from Poland and even farther realms. Each one sought the dragon's cave, and each one perished before even landing a blow on the wicked wyrm's scaly flesh.

At last a humble shoemaker's son named Krak approached the king and asked permission to try to slay the serpent. The king was skeptical because Krak had no horse, no armor, and no weapon beyond his sharp leatherworking knife. But when the young man said that he had a new plan, the monarch agreed to let him try and offered him the help of his realm's tradesmen.

Krak asked for a dead sheep, freshly killed, from a butcher. From the many miners who worked their tunnels in the hills above the Vistula River he acquired a good-sized bag of sulphur. Cutting open the sheep's belly with his knife, Krak stuffed the sack of sulphur in between the animal's ribs. That evening he carried the dead sheep to the mouth of the cave. He set the carcass down on a dry patch of ground and took shelter behind a large rock on a little knoll above the water.

At sunset, the dragon emerged from its cave. Immediately it spotted the sheep, and with a snap of its great jaws it gulped down the offering. Almost immediately it belched a great cloud of yellow smoke and uttered a roar of pain—as Krak had intended, the sulphur caught fire, ignited by the heat of the wyrm's own infernal gut. The dragon dropped its head into the river and began to drink, gulping down gallons of water, uttering gurgling gasps as the water mixed with the fiery sulphur and turned to steam. Finally, the pressure within the monster grew too great, and its vast, swollen belly literally exploded in a blast of hot coals and steam.

Krak entered the cave, filled a sack with treasures from the dragon's hoard, and then departed to tell the king of his success. When the ruler sent a party of armed men to investigate, they reported that the lad was telling the truth. Overjoyed, the king gave his daughter to the dragonslayer, who—because of the treasure he'd recovered—was now a wealthy man. People returned to the land around Wawel Hill, which had not been farmed for some years, and found that it was fertile and good for grazing.

When the old king died, Krak ascended to the throne and built a castle atop the hill. For centuries that castle served as the seat of the Polish crown. The city that grew up around it was named Krakow, after the hero who made it possible.

A HERO REMEMBERED

A monument to Krak's dragon still stands near the cave at the foot of Wawel Hill. The monument includes a statue of the dragon, which contains a feed of natural gas that allows the statue to belch a cloud of fiery breath several times per hour.

Dragons of Southern Slavic Realms

In regions such as Bulgaria and Croatia, dragon myths took on a different tone from those of Russia and places farther north. In the south, dragons were considered to be very wise beings that were not necessarily enemies of humankind. They could use magic spells, and sometimes, if approached in the right way, they would share their knowledge.

These dragons were presumed to dwell in remote hills. Often their treasures included unique and magical objects. It was not uncommon for one of these dragons to lust after a beautiful human woman—nor were these attentions always unwelcome. Some of the great heroes of these cultures were said to be the offspring of a draconic father and a human mother.

SON OF THE DRAGON

The Carpathian Mountains, mentioned previously in this chapter, were also home to one of the most famous monsters of legend: Count Dracula. Bram Stoker's 1897 novel *Dracula* established the general boundaries of this legend. Stoker was probably influenced in his choice of names for his villain by the career of Vlad III, prince of Wallachia, a member of the house of Drăculești. Vlad was inducted into the Order of the Dragon, a chivalric order that had been founded in 1408. Dracula can be translated as "son of the dragon."

CHAPTER 7

DRAGONS
of Other
Cultural Myths

lthough most of our most famous tales of dragons come to us
from the ancient cultures of the vast Eurasian land mass, the
giant serpent as ally and adversary is a universal feature of the
beliefs of human tribes and cultures around the world. Statues,
paintings, mosaics, legends, and myths from around the world provide ample
proof that the concept of the dragon as an exalted serpent is universal.

Dragon Myths of the Western Hemisphere

A creature much like a dragon was imagined by the early Americans who
dwelt, and formed substantial towns, along the Mississippi River in the central United States. Farther south, a dragon as a creator god was universally

worshipped, and portrayed in mosaic, glyph, and statuary among the peoples of both the Mexican heartland and the Mayan forests of southern Mexico and Central America. That dragon, Quetzalcoatl, is arguably the most important and visible image associated with pre-Columbian Mesoamerica.

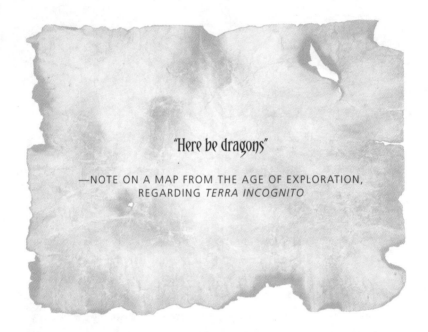

"Here be dragons"

—NOTE ON A MAP FROM THE AGE OF EXPLORATION, REGARDING *TERRA INCOGNITO*

The Piasa

The accounts of this creature, described as a dragon with the face of a man and a tail that was twice the length of a man's height, come from the Algonquin tribes of what is now the central United States. Though these tribes did not develop writing before their encounters with Europeans, they did inscribe a detailed image of the Piasa on a large shelf of limestone rock above the Mississippi River, in what would become Madison County, Illinois. The original artwork was—unbelievably—destroyed in the 1870s because the Mississippi Lime Company quarried away the stone.

Still, the work was seen and described by the first European explorer known to have passed that way, the Jesuit priest Father Jacques Marquette. His account of the images is vivid:

> *"Two painted monsters . . . large as a calf . . . they have Horns on their heads Like those of a deer, a horrible look, red eyes, a beard Like a tiger's, a face somewhat like a man's, a body Covered with scales, and so Long A tail that it winds all around the Body, passing above the head and going back between the legs, ending in a Fish's tail. Green, red, and black are the three Colors composing the Picture. Moreover, these 2 monsters are so well painted that we cannot believe that any savage is their author; for good painters in France would find it difficult to reach that place Conveniently to paint them."*

The painting was probably created by natives of the city of Cahokia, perhaps around the year 1200. Cahokia is believed to have been the largest city north of Mexico prior to the coming of the Europeans, with as many as 30,000 residents. Many other types of animals, including hawks, bird-men, and gigantic snakes, were commonly portrayed by the people of Cahokia. But the Piasa, with its draconic appearance and prominent position—it could be readily viewed by anyone making his way up or down the "father of waters" past that point—was a unique and dramatic statement of Native American artistry.

Very little is known of the creature, except that the original painting was supposed to represent the Piasa in its actual size. It may well have been a warning, or at least a signpost, informing travelers that they were entering the tribal holdings of a very powerful chiefdom.

Avan Yu (Awanyu)

Featured as a painting on walls and as a motif in Native American pottery, the Avan Yu is a serpent god considered to be a guardian of water. Mostly seen in caves near rivers in New Mexico and Arizona, the serpent's body is always represented by flowing curves that seem to suggest water or waves. It has one, two, or three horns upon its head, and its tongue is associated with a lightning bolt. Because of the locations where the images have been found, always near rivers, it is clear that the Avan Yu symbolized the importance of running water to those peoples who dwelt in the desert and depended on the rivers for their survival.

Quetzalcoatl: The Feathered Dragon

From the area south of the great Mexican desert, extending through the savannah of the Yucatan peninsula and into the rain forest of the land bridge now known as Central America, great civilizations flourished long before the coming of the Europeans. The Toltecs, Aztecs, Mayans, and others differed from each other in many respects, but they all held one thing in common: a belief that a great, feathered dragon god formed a central pillar of their very existence. This powerful, fearsome deity was universally known as Quetzalcoatl—commonly pronounced *ketz-al-co-AH-tel*.

Often called the Plumed Serpent, Quetzalcoatl is portrayed in sculpture and mosaic as being a huge snake with a crown of bright feathers around a fanged and fearsome head. In many of these depictions, feathers and plumage adorn the coiling, serpentine body, including a tail branching into numerous trailing strands. In one famous image painted after the Spanish conquest, he appears on a mural with his vast jaws gaping wide as he devours a whole host of men.

A Creator God from the Distant Past

In the Mesoamerican view of the world, the earth was currently in its fifth incarnation—The Fifth Sun—having been destroyed in each of its earlier forms by battles between the gods. Quetzalcoatl played a prominent role in

the mythology of each of these ages. The Feathered Dragon was one of the primary gods of the cosmos, a direct descendant of the original creator, and master of one of the four quarters of the compass, the west. The evening star, Venus, glimmered as his brilliant symbol, and the Plumed Serpent helped to form the boundary between the earth and the sky.

Quetzalcoatl was one of four sons of the original god, Ometeotl. Ometeotl created his four sons and then more or less retired from active participation in the affairs of the world. The sons, each a mighty god, formed the current earth, atmosphere, seas, and the underworld—known as Mictlan. Having created the firmament, all four of the brother gods worked together to lift the sun into the sky.

But only the Plumed Serpent, Quetzalcoatl, entered the underworld to gather the pieces of humanity—including bits of monkeys, giants, and others—that had been lost in the previous destructive events. Quetzalcoatl brought those components to the surface. He pierced his own body in his tongue, nostrils, and genitals, using the blood he shed to form those pieces into humans. Thus he was the god who created man.

THE BENEFICENCE OF THE GOD

It is telling that in a religious ethos that created and idolized a great many brutal and bloodthirsty gods, the feathered dragon remained a beneficent force in the eyes of his peoples. They credited him with bringing maize (corn) to the world. He aided fertility and contributed to good weather—always a god of light, wind, and mercy.

A Dragon of Many Faces

Although Quetzalcoatl's most impressive visage was that of the mighty plumed serpent, with devouring jaws and a long, plumed tail, he was also capable of appearing in the guise of a man. He controlled the wind and air, and in yet another magical form he swirled about as the god of wind, Ehecatl. Indeed, the temples erected in Ehecatl's honor tended to be round—the only such temples in Mesoamerica—so that they had no flat walls or corners to obstruct the flow of air.

LEGENDS OF HIS FALL

Quetzalcoatl was famed for his enduring conflict with another, darker god known as Tezcatlipoca—a master of night, deceit, sorcery, and the earth itself. Tezcatlipoca stood in natural opposition to the Plumed Serpent's mastery of the air. The two mightiest of the four brothers who raised the sun into the heavens, they were sworn enemies.

As a god of trickery, Tezcatlipoca created a fatal trap for Quetzalcoatl by deceiving his brother into consuming strong drink. In his maddened intoxication, the Plumed Serpent had sex with a celibate goddess who was also his sister. Awakening and consumed by guilt, Quetzalcoatl resolved to depart from the world of man.

In one version of the myth the feathered dragon built a great fire and then flew into the flames to self-destruction. Another tale has him, in response to his great shame, abandoning Mexico and sailing off to the east on a raft of snakes, with a promise to return, for good or ill, at some point in the future. The day of his departure was represented on the calendar as "One Reed," a fact that had significant ramifications with the coming of the Spanish conquistadores.

Throughout the eras of his domain—and as evidence of his essentially good nature—the Plumed Serpent was also heralded as the creator of the calendar and writing. He was a patron of priests, and in several cultures high priests assumed his name. One of the societies that supplanted the Toltecs (but predated the Aztecs) actually referred to their rulers as "Quetzalcoatl."

The Plumed Serpent and the Conquest of Mexico

In 1519 the Spanish explorer and conqueror Hernán Cortés landed on the coast of Mexico near the site of the modern city of Vera Cruz. Drawn by reports of a great city of gold and fascinated and appalled by the bestial statues and bloody sacrifices of the Aztecs, Cortés led his men inland toward the Aztec capital, Tenochtitlan. Along the way, they beheld images of Quetzalcoatl, with his fanged visage and bright plumage.

The Aztecs horrified the Spanish with their massive rituals of human sacrifice. Even though Quetzalcoatl was not a deity worshiped by human sacrifice, the fanged, flying serpent replete with bright plumage matched the contemporary Christian interpretation of dragons and helped to convince the conquistadores that they were doing God's work against the followers of a

wicked creature, clearly symbolic of Satan's power. Of course, such a rationale also helped to justify their plundering of the vast hoard of pure, precious gold.

The Spanish arrived at Tenochtitlan on the calendar day of One Reed. Perhaps some of the Aztecs, and their leader Moctezuma, had come to believe that Cortés was in fact Quetzalcoatl—in his human guise—returning to the land he had departed in an earlier age. Certainly, this helps explain how such a small group of invaders at first paralyzed the Aztec leadership into inactivity and soon completed the utter conquest of the most powerful and militant nation of the New World.

In fact, part of the legend of Quetzalcoatl's fall suggested that he would return and bring ruin to that world. By the end of Cortés's campaign of conquest, a bare two years later, Spanish artillery had blasted the magnificent Aztec capital of Tenochtitlan into rubble. Huge numbers of the native population had perished from the previously unknown scourge of smallpox. It is easy to see how the myth and the prophecy of the Feathered Dragon combined to bring about the ruin of Mesoamerican society—and led very directly into the almost complete conversion of the people to Christianity.

Dragon Myths of Sub-Saharan Africa

Dahomey

Dahomey was an African kingdom (located, roughly, in the current Republic of Benin) that was the center of a cult of serpent worship. At the ritual center of Whydah stood a temple in which lived some fifty snakes. The python seemed to be the central breed and was highly venerated. This serpentine deity is sometimes regarded as a version of the Rainbow Serpent, which was worshiped in other parts of Africa, including the Congo and Nigeria. The faith in serpents was carried to Haiti, where elements of it survive in the practice of vodou (voodoo).

The Rainbow Serpent was a giant python central to the mythologies of many different cultures. It was a water serpent, living in mud during dry seasons, and was said to be benign and friendly toward humans.

Ethiopian Dream Dragon

This dragon legend describes huge creatures that lived in the mountains of Ethiopia. Each had four wings and two clawed feet. These dragons were large enough to hunt and eat elephants and had vile, poisonous breath—made all the more lethal by their tendency to seek out and consume toxic plants. One story about the Ethiopian dragons claims that several of them twisted themselves together "like willow tree branches" so that they could make themselves into a seagoing raft. They then launched themselves into the sea and sailed as far as Arabia, where they sought fresh sources of food.

The Amphisbaena

This mythical beast was originally native to Libya. The name means "going in both directions." It is typically portrayed as a serpent that had a head at each end of its long, coiling body, the latter of which was covered with scales. It was described for posterity by the famed Roman scribe Pliny the Elder. Another similar creature was said to inhabit unexplored islands in the southern half of the world; the amphisbaena of those regions were believed to have a shelled body like a turtle's, but also with two heads.

The amphisbaena could run in either direction at full speed. Some illustrations portrayed the animal with wings, though it seems likely those wings were for show—it was not supposed to be capable of actual flight. However, the creature could take one neck in the mouth of the opposite head, forming a hoop that allowed it to roll quickly over the ground. When the female amphisbaena watched over her eggs, she was able to keep one of the heads awake at all times so that the nest would never go unguarded. The creature's eyes shone as bright as oil lamps, and it was unaffected by cold. It was said to be poisonous from one or both of its mouths and capable of uttering a loud hiss when aroused. At least one legend suggests that the skin of an amphisbaena, if found after the serpent had sloughed it off, could be wrapped by a person around a walking stick and would ward off all snakes and other creatures that kill not by biting but by striking.

THE GORGON'S BLOOD

According to the Greeks, when the hero Jason had slain the Gorgon, Medusa (whose hair was writhing snakes and whose gaze could turn men to stone), he cut off her head and carried it with him as he flew over the Mediterranean on winged sandals. Blood from the severed head dripped on the sands of Libya, creating the amphisbaena.

"One two! One two!

And through and through

The vorpal blade went snicker-snack!

He left it dead, and with its head

He went galumphing back.

'And, hast thou slain the Jabberwock?

Come to my arms, my beamish boy!

O frabjous day! Callooh! Callay!'

He chortled in his joy."

—LEWIS CARROLL,
EXCERPT FROM "JABBERWOCKY"

PART III

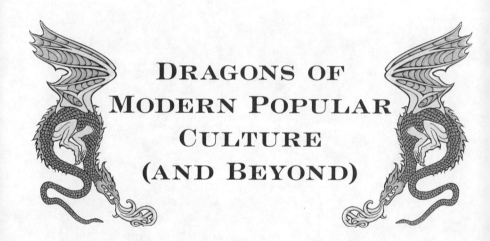

DRAGONS OF MODERN POPULAR CULTURE (AND BEYOND)

CHAPTER 8

NOTABLE DRAGONS
of Popular Fiction

 ewis Carroll, in his poem "Jabberwocky," never mentions the word "dragon"—in fact part of the poem's delight is that he makes up words and employs them in such a way that we, the reader, know exactly what he means. Nevertheless, "Jabberwocky" is a whimsical tale of a dragonslayer, and the poet gives us enough detail—"the jaws that bite, the claws that catch"—that the reader can vividly picture the action. This is how universal the dragon myth is in our minds and in our literature.

In this part, we look at a small sample of popular books that feature dragons as characters and antagonists. It is not possible to examine all the novels, stories, poems, or series that focus on, let along mention or include, dragons. For this reason, we have picked out some notable examples of the genre, which should give you some ideas for where you might turn for inspiration.

Smaug: Terror under the Mountain

Sometimes known as Smaug the Magnificent or Smaug the Golden, this terrible serpent embodies all that is frightful in the classic image of the dragon in the Western world. Depicted by fantasy master J. R. R. Tolkien in *The Hobbit*, Smaug was huge and already centuries old when he flew down from the north of Middle-Earth seeking the legendary treasure hoard collected by the dwarves of Erebor, the Lonely Mountain.

For generations those doughty miners and smiths had excavated precious metals and brilliant gemstones from the depths underneath Middle-Earth. They created a great kingdom and were so prosperous that humans came to live outside of the mountain, establishing the thriving city of Dale, with a toy market known far and wide for its wondrous trinkets. The master craftsmanship of the dwarves was worth a lot to the humans, and the profits of that work only added to the vast holdings of dwarvenkind.

Thror was King under the Mountain in those days, and a great ruler he was, and very, very rich. But wicked and powerful dragons are drawn to such wealth, and Smaug was undoubtedly the most wicked and powerful dragon of his time. He flew down from the northern wilderness to attack, landing first on top of the mountain and setting its forests aflame with his breath. The dwarven army formed ranks and charged out of the mountain's gate to do battle, and in those ranks they died, a host of bold warriors charred and smashed by the dragon's wrath.

The waters of the river flowing from the mountain rose in a great cloud of steam, and from this steam Smaug emerged to assail the army of Dale, killing most of the human warriors in the first clash of battle. Then the dragon crashed through the front gate of the dwarven kingdom, wrecked the great halls, and killed any dwarves who dared to remain. A very few survivors, including the king and his son, escaped through a secret door, while the king's grandson, Thorin, happened to be outside at the time of the attack and could only watch in horror as his ancestral realm was pillaged.

For 150 years Smaug dwelt under the mountain, gathering all his baubles into a great pile and sleeping on those treasures in such torpor that many gems became embedded in his belly, adding to the armored protection of his scales. In the early years after the sacking of the mountain, he emerged to attack the humans who still remained in Dale, often carrying away maidens to devour, until finally the people abandoned that charred city, and all the land around the mountain became a barren waste. Smaug might have remained there forever, if not for the courage—reckless heroism, actually—of a small band of unlikely adventurers.

The leader of these adventurers was the wizard, Gandalf the Gray, who in his wisdom knew that a dark age was arising in Middle-Earth, and feared that Smaug would become an agent of that darkness. He was willingly aided by thirteen dwarves, including Thorin, the grandson of the former King under the Mountain. The final member of the party, perhaps not as eager as the rest but no less heroic for his grasp of common sense, was Bilbo

Baggins, a hobbit of the Shire. These fifteen made their way past many perils and adventures, entering the mountain by a secret door. It was Bilbo who spotted the lone weakness of the dragon, an area of his breast unprotected by the gemstone coat of armor.

Smaug's wrath was aroused by the intrusion, and he emerged to attack the adventurers and the warriors of nearby Laketown. One of these warriors was a human archer, Bard, of great skill, and when he learned of the dragon's weakness he fired a lethal arrow. That weapon pierced the dragon's scaly belly and drove all the way into his heart, killing him, and finally freeing the land around the Lonely Mountain from the dragon's terrible reign.

AN EXPERT AUTHOR

When Oxford professor J. R. R. Tolkien wrote *The Hobbit* (published in 1937), he was already famed as a master of early English literature, and the lore of myth and legend that underlay so much of modern European history. His analysis of the early poem *Beowulf*, with its own fire-breathing dragon, is still considered to be important. It is not surprising that Tolkien's novel introduced a dragon so wicked and powerful that it encapsulated a great deal of earlier myth and became an archetype for modern fantasy fiction.

The Dragons of Earthsea

The archipelago of Earthsea is home to humans who can use magic and to many fantastic beings as well, including a thriving population of dragons. Created by author Ursula K. Le Guin, Earthsea was the setting for six novels. In the creation myth of the world, in fact, humans and dragons were considered to be the same race. However, serpents chose the freedom offered by fire and air; the humans elected, instead, to serve the material masters of water and earth.

During the time of the Earthsea stories, the dragons are established in their own realm, at the western edge of the archipelago. They do, however, make raids to claim food and treasure from the realms of humans. Most humans cannot resist or fight dragons, but the few who became wizards have the power to stand up to dragons; it is the wizards who keep dragonkind from running roughshod over all the islands.

Dragons in this world are not inherently good or evil but are rather aloof from the affairs of men—and always they are dangerous. Since dragons live for many centuries, they consider humans to be insignificant and immature, not worthy of interest. Dragonspeech occurs in the Language of the Making, an ancient tongue that only dragons can master. A few human wizards, however, achieve the exalted status of dragonlords, and they can actually speak a rudimentary form of the language, allowing them to communicate with dragons.

A NEW TAKE ON FANTASY

Ursula K. Le Guin created one of the most enduring fictional fantasy realms in the 1960s when she began the Earthsea series. The series consists of six novels and several short stories, with the first stories published in 1964, and the first novel—*A Wizard of Earthsea*—in 1968. Unlike much of earlier fantasy fiction, Le Guin's stories are notable for the importance and power of some of the female characters.

Dragons of Pern

The wildly popular series Dragons of Pern takes a unique view of dragons, as the author Anne McCaffrey develops the epic saga through no less than two dozen books. Although humans ride the backs of fire-breathing dragons on the world of Pern, the series is actually a science fiction, not a fantasy, story. There is no use of, or belief in, magic or supernatural abilities in these books; rather, the dragons have been genetically modified to perform a specific function on their world.

The planet Pern was colonized by space-faring humans many centuries ago. It suffers from a unique and dangerous phenomenon, something that happens only once every few centuries. A plague of precipitation, called Thread, falls from the sky with terrible destructive force, chemically scorching and consuming organic material, including flesh. The dragons of Pern were created by the human settlers specifically to deal with this threat, which lasts for a span of about fifty years, followed by two centuries of Thread-free safety.

The early settlers of Pern bred their dragons from the fire lizards native to the planet. As dragons, they are powerful and serpentine, flying with the power of two broad wings, and capable of breathing fire. This fire can destroy the Thread in the air before it has a chance to land and destroy.

Pern's dragons look very much like the classic dragons of Western mythology. However, they have smooth, leathery skin instead of scales. They grow quickly, achieving full size in about a year and a half. Each dragon, shortly after it hatches from an egg, will imprint upon the first thing—usually a human—that feeds it. A dragon and its rider thus form a bond that lasts a lifetime. The genetic code of the Pern dragons has been designed to make them receptive to human commands, and a dragon in most cases willingly obeys the wishes of its rider.

Pern dragons have telepathic abilities allowing them to communicate with their riders and with other nearby dragons. They also have the ability to teleport to anyplace on the world—and sometimes even through time—by "going between." They transport themselves and their riders, as well as anything being carried by the dragon, to a chilly sort of void; after several seconds, they emerge from "between" at their intended destination. If a dragon's rider dies, the dragon will typically commit suicide by going between, then failing to emerge in any location.

The Serpents of the Dragon Knight

Beginning with *The Dragon and the George* in 1976, the Dragon Knight series by Gordon R. Dickson is a lighthearted but detail-rich fantasy about a modern couple, Jim and Angie, who are magically transported to medieval England—but it is an alternate England, in which magic and dragons are real. So real, in fact, that Jim arrives in the past in the actual form of a dragon. Angie, however, remains a human—but she, in turn, is captured by the "Dark Powers" and locked away in the Loathly Tower.

One of the fascinating aspects of the first book of the series is that it is told from the point of view of Jim as a dragon. He learns the limitations of his strength and is counseled by knights and magic users; eventually, with the aid of loyal friends he is able to rescue Angie and return to his human form. As the series continues, the couple decides to remain in their medieval world, where Jim has won a barony that includes a small castle and its holdings.

Some of the delights in the stories come from Dickson's details of mundane life in the Middle Ages, including factors such as bedbugs, lice, and dysentery, as well as pragmatic chores like getting the moat drained. There is also an Accounting Office of Magic that exerts a great deal of control over wizards and dragons. Jim—sometimes willingly, sometimes by command of the Accounting Office—frequently returns to dragon form as he goes about a series of imaginative tasks.

The Saga of Dragonlance

The world of Krynn, created by Margaret Weis and Tracy Hickman in 1984 and supplemented by numerous other authors, is a fantasy homeland, rich with history, to a broad variety of citizenry, including humans, dwarves, elves, and many others. It is also the home, and the domain, to many species of dragons. The great serpents of Krynn represent both sides of the moral spectrum: Colored dragons (red, green, black, blue, and white) serve the five-headed Queen of Darkness, the goddess Takhisis; while metallic dragons (copper, brass, bronze, silver, and gold) acknowledge the great platinum dragon, Paladine, as their master.

The stories of Krynn include more than 190 novels. The first three— *Dragons of Autumn Twilight*; *Dragons of Winter Night*; and *Dragons of Spring Dawning*—relate the epic of how dragons, once thought lost from the world, returned. The first to arrive were the evil dragons serving the Queen of Darkness. Ridden by armored knights and highlords, these dragons flew in the vanguard of the queen's invading armies as they swept across the world, bringing chaos and destruction with them, until only a very few lands remained free of their control.

With the courageous intervention of a few brave heroes, the metallic dragons were released from exile and returned, just in the nick of time, to give the forces of virtue a fighting chance. The knights who ride the good dragons arm themselves with potent dragonlances, magically forged weapons that inflict terrible wounds upon the dragons. With these lethal arms in their arsenal, the riders and their metallic dragons wage a campaign in the skies against the Dark Queen's vile wyrms, and the future of the world's people is given hope.

Later novels detail the world of Krynn, both before and after the War of the Lance. A number of writers have shared the creation of these stories, making Krynn perhaps the most elaborately detailed "shared world" in the realm of fantasy fiction.

A GAME WORLD IN FICTION

The world of Krynn, the setting for the Dragonlance stories, was originally created by the game designers of TSR, Inc. as a location for *Dungeons & Dragons* adventures. Tracy Hickman, the lead game designer, and Margaret Weis, of the company's book department, together wrote the first Dragonlance novels, which became a major commercial success and opened the new field of game-based fiction. An exhaustive series of detailed game products published by TSR (and later Wizards of the Coast and Margaret Weis Productions) maps out the world and includes descriptions of the dragons, as well as other creatures and characters that live there.

Dragons of Harry Potter's World

As befitting a fantasy environment as broad and all-encompassing as that created by author J. K. Rowling for her epic, and incredibly popular, series about Harry Potter, the English boy who discovers that he is a wizard, the world of Hogwarts includes several important references to a variety of dragons. While these serpents are not central to the story, they provide vivid examples of the author's imagination and the sense of peril and adventure that reverberate so vividly through the seven books of the Harry Potter series.

Guardians of Gringotts

The central wizarding bank is an ancient establishment, called Gringotts, established and run by goblins. The treasures that witches and wizards wish to secure in the vaults of this highly reputable institution are secured in a labyrinthine maze of subterranean corridors reached by wildly careening carts running along a network of rails. Many magical protections secure these hoards, but a more traditional method of treasure guarding is also employed by the goblins of Gringotts: dragons.

Obstacles in a Contest

The most detailed description of the various types of dragons in the world of Harry Potter occurs during an episode in *Harry Potter and the Goblet of Fire*. Four students are competing in a series of magical tests to obtain the goblet, and the first test requires the student to steal a golden orb from the possession of an angry, untamed dragon. The four types of dragons are the Common Welsh Green, the Swedish Short-Snout, the Chinese Fireball, and— the nastiest tempered and most dangerous one—the Hungarian Horntail.

THE TYPES OF DRAGONS

In *Fantastic Beasts and Where to Find Them*, Newt Scamander details (among other things) the dragons that are to be found in Harry Potter's world. They include:

- The Antipodean Opaleye
- The Chinese Fireball
- The Common Welsh Green
- The Hebridean Black
- The Hungarian Horntail
- The Norwegian Ridgeback
- The Peruvian Vipertooth
- The Romanian Longhorn
- The Swedish Short-Snout
- The Ukrainian Ironbelly
- The Catalonian Fireball
- The Portuguese Long-Snout

CHAPTER 9

NOTABLE
DRAGONS
of Film

trait of all dragons in all cultures is that they inspire awe in anyone who sees one. Because film is a visual medium, it lends itself to this sense of awe, whether it be horror or inspiration. Many notable films have portrayed dragons, most typically as powerful monsters.

Through the middle of the twentieth century dragons were rendered either by an artist, such as in Walt Disney's epic *Sleeping Beauty*, or through stop-motion animation of the type employed by famed special effects genius Ray Harryhausen in movies like *The Seven Voyages of Sinbad*.

As computerized special effects technology continues to improve, the possibilities for fabulous special effects have gotten exponentially better. Naturally, special effects featuring dragons have created some of the most memorable images in modern filmmaking.

As with books, it would be impossible to describe every dragon ever included in a movie, but this chapter presents a representative sample of some of the most dramatic, emphasizing those available for viewing today.

"Never tickle a sleeping dragon."
(The motto of Hogwarts School of
Witchcraft and Wizardry.)

—J. K. ROWLING

Dragons in Animated Films

In the early years of color movies, the power of animation was turned into movie magic, most notably by Walt Disney and his studio. Each frame of his films was drawn by hand. In the modern era, animated films are still created by human artists, though computerized equipment is used to make the pictures move smoothly. Regardless, animation can create memorable and terrifying images of the great serpents we know as dragons.

Sleeping Beauty

Made by Walt Disney studios in 1959, this fairy tale-turned-film is the last of what might be called "first generation" Disney animated tales. The movie is not about a dragon, but the villainous Maleficent is a wicked fairy with a witch-like persona and the sorcerous ability to change her shape. In the climactic scene of the movie, she transforms into a spectacularly huge and powerful dragon. She drives the handsome Prince Phillip to the very edge of a steep cliff, breathing fire, roaring, flapping her massive wings. When it looks like the prince is doomed, however, a trio of helpful fairies put a blessing on his great sword. He throws the weapon, which strikes the dragon in the heart, destroying Maleficent and setting up happy endings all around.

The Flight of Dragons

This film was a major animated release in 1982. The plot centers on a world where magic is fading because of the rise of science, and four wizards—each of whom has a powerful dragon for a companion—meet to create a plan to preserve their powers in at least one, limited realm. Naturally, the wizards squabble and the Red Wizard seeks to control all the others.

A knight and a dragon set out on a quest to defeat the evil wizard. They are joined by Peter, a man who has been magically transported from the modern world. Peter is aided by a shield that can deflect magic and a flute that has the power to put dragons to sleep. Magic goes awry and Peter finds his mind transferred into the body of a dragon. He stumbles about making a mess of things, until he is aided by a mature dragon who mentors him about life in a draconic form.

Magic and science contrast nicely in the movie, as Peter's scientific knowledge comes in handy for *some* things, while sorcery and enchantment help in other ways. Eventually the questers must face an entire army of dragons serving the evil wizard, but—with the aid of the magic flute—good triumphs over evil. Peter is returned to his normal form, and his normal time, and the last dragons finally get to retire to the realm where magic still lives.

Shrek and Its Sequels

This wonderful film, released in 2001 by PDI/DreamWorks, is not focused on a dragon. However, the dragon—called, simply, "Dragon"—in the movie plays a significant role and is characterized with such pathos that it really deserves mention in any discussion of notable dragons in movies.

The movie pokes fun at many aspects of fairy tales and, especially, of the "Disney" view of storytelling and the marketing of its product. Dragon's role in this movie is to guard a princess who has been locked high in a tower. The princess is compelled by magic to wait for the stalwart hero who will rescue her and then claim her heart with "love's first kiss."

Shrek, a gruff ogre seeking only to get his precious swamp back to himself, finds himself required to rescue the princess. Accompanied by his faithful, but annoying, talking donkey—naturally, named "Donkey"—he penetrates the castle and climbs the tower to rescue the princess. Donkey, meanwhile, encounters the dragon, discovers she is a female, and flirts with her long enough for Shrek to come back and rescue him. Shrek and Donkey's subsequent escape, with the princess, is a harrowing chase through a maze-like castle, with lots of fiery dragon breath hurrying them along. With a little cleverness, the ogre manages to tether the dragon to a chain that is just short enough to allow the trio to escape only slightly singed.

At that point the story might have left the dragon behind . . . except that Donkey, after a falling out with Shrek, finds the lovesick dragon pining for him in the wilderness. The two become friends, Donkey makes up with Shrek, and the two of them ride the dragon to the castle of the wicked king, arriving just in time to stop the princess from making a terrible mistake. Here again the dragon plays a key role, thwarting the king's plan permanently with one giant gulp.

Dragon makes a brief appearance at the end of *Shrek 2*, as Donkey pines for the beloved mate he left behind to embark on that movie's adventure. Dragon shows up with a whole brood of tiny winged, fire-breathing "dronkeys," and Donkey learns he is a proud papa. In *Shrek the Third*, the dragon also has a small part. At the end of the movie, she pushes over Rapunzel's tower to crush the villain, Prince Charming.

How to Train Your Dragon

Released by DreamWorks in 2010, this film offers an amazing number of splendidly realized dragons. The story is set in an imaginary Viking village named Berk, where the citizens have been engaged in a long battle against swarms of dragons that relentlessly attack and carry off the Viking's livestock and other food supplies. Dragon fighting, consequently, is a skill highly prized by the people of Berk.

The chief of the village is a burly Viking named Stoick the Vast, who is rather embarrassed by the clumsiness of his awkward son, a young teenager named Hiccup. Hiccup tries to earn some respect during a dragon attack when he shoots and hits a rare kind of dragon called a Night Fury, but nobody sees him do it. Hiccup tracks the wounded dragon into the forest but doesn't have the heart to administer the killing blow. Instead, Hiccup gradually befriends the dragon, naming the creature "Toothless" because of his retractable teeth.

Hiccup eventually makes a prosthetic tail that will allow Toothless to fly again, and the boy also designs a harness that allows him to ride the dragon and steer it in flight. At the same time, Stoick has ordered Hiccup to take a dragon-killing class, while the chieftain leads the Viking fleet off to seek the dragons' home lair. Because of what he learns from Toothless, Hiccup does very well in the class, to the annoyance of Astrid, a village girl he secretly likes. These scenes also introduce a sort of catalogue of dragons, with many types described, leading up to the horrid Monstrous Nightmare.

Stoick and the Viking fleet, much the worse for wear, return home in failure. Astrid follows Hiccup into the woods and discovers Toothless. She wants to tell everyone Hiccup's secret, but he pulls her onto the dragon's back and the Night Fury takes them for a ride. The girl's fear soon turns to delight as they soar through the skies.

However, Toothless turns to join a great swarm of dragons, bearing the two helpless young people along as all the serpents fly to an island. There they see the Red Death, a massive dragon that has enslaved all the others, forcing them to bring it food or be eaten themselves. They agree to keep the lair a secret, to protect Toothless.

However, the existence of the tame dragon is dramatically revealed when Toothless flies into the village to save Hiccup from a dangerous threat. Stoick, enraged, captures Toothless and disowns his son. Having learned of the island lair, the Viking chief is determined to use Toothless to lead him there; once more he departs with the replenished fleet.

Knowing his father is sailing into disaster, with a helpless Toothless captive on his ship, Hiccup and the other students from the dragon-killing class follow the fleet to try and prevent catastrophe. Freeing Toothless, Hiccup mounts his dragon and takes to the air, distracting the Red Death before it can destroy the Viking fleet. The brave pair lures the huge serpent into a lethal dive, just barely escaping before the massive wyrm smashes into the ground and explodes.

Hiccup and Toothless are hailed as heroes and the war between the Vikings and dragons at last comes to an end.

HOW TO TRAIN YOUR DRAGON BOOKS

There are ten books in the How to Train Your Dragon series, written by the British author Cressida Cowell. These books detail the further adventures of Hiccup, Toothless, and the Vikings as they battle other foes, both dragon and human.

Dragons in Nonanimated Films

The 7th Voyage of Sinbad

This imaginative fantasy was released by Columbia Pictures in 1958. The special effects were brilliantly rendered through stop-motion filming of models. Though dragons are not central to the story, two serpentine creatures play significant roles. One of these is a female nāga, a woman with four arms and a long snake's body who performs an elaborate dance before the Caliph of Baghdad, Sinbad, and others at a great wedding feast.

After adventures with a Cyclops, a roc, a genie, and others, Sinbad must sneak past a chained dragon as he enters the cave of a wicked sorcerer. He subsequently releases the dragon when he needs it to battle a pursuing Cyclops. When the sorcerer sends the dragon flying after Sinbad's ship, the captain's sailors construct a giant crossbow and fire an arrow at the flying serpent. Mortally wounded, it falls upon the wicked sorcerer and kills him.

Pete's Dragon

Made in 1977, this is a live-action movie with an animated dragon. Produced by Walt Disney's studio, it is a children's movie and was later made into a musical. Set about a hundred years ago, it features a young orphan, Pete, who is fleeing a comically abusive hillbilly family. The family, who paid $50 for the orphan boy, pursues to get him back. Pete is mysteriously saved from capture by an invisible force.

That force turns out to be a huge dragon named Elliot who has the power to make himself vanish. Many complications ensue as Pete finds himself in a small seaside town. His efforts to fit in are made difficult by Elliot's clumsiness, though he is invisible for most of his antics, so people simply view Pete as a source of bad luck.

Gradually, however, a few people—both good and bad—figure out that Elliot is real. A traveling snake oil salesman tries to buy the dragon from Pete so that he can make potions and concoctions out of parts of the serpent's body, but the boy won't sell. The lighthouse keeper and his daughter have been friendly to Pete, and when the light goes out in the middle of a climactic storm, Elliot's fiery breath reignites it and saves the day. Pete finds a place to live and Elliot says goodbye, telling his friend he now needs to go and find another child who needs his help.

Dragonslayer

The product of a 1981 partnership between Walt Disney and Paramount, this film used some sixteen different puppets—including one forty feet long—to portray the great serpent at the heart of the movie. The special effects were handled by Industrial Light and Magic, which had established its great reputation with movies such as *Star Wars* and *Raiders of the Lost Ark*.

Set in a sixth-century kingdom during the Dark Ages after the fall of Rome, the story introduces a four-hundred-year-old wyrm named Vermithrax Pejorative. Urland's king appeases it by offering it a virgin girl, chosen by lottery, as a sacrifice every six months. Since the situation cannot continue indefinitely, the king sends an expedition to try and recruit the world's last sorcerer to come to Urland and deal with the dragon. When the group finds the sorcerer, he boasts that he is invulnerable, and a thuggish soldier, Tyrian, stabs the wizard to test him. The old sorcerer dies instantly, much to the horror of his apprentice Galen.

Galen cremates his master's body and carries the ashes and the wizard's amulet with him as he journeys to Urland. He learns that the wizard wanted his ashes to be spread across "burning water." During the journey, Galen learns that one of the king's loyal soldiers, Valerian, is actually a young woman who has disguised herself as a man to avoid the lottery. She tells him that the lottery is rigged so that the king's daughter will never be chosen.

In Urland, Galen attempts to seal the dragon in its lair by bringing down a landslide across the cavern mouth. Tyrian apprehends the apprentice and drags him before the king, who fears that Galen has merely angered the wyrm, not killed it. He takes the amulet away from the young man and orders him imprisoned. The haughty princess comes to mock him, but when he tells her that the lottery is rigged, she confronts her father, and he admits that she cannot be chosen.

In the meantime, the dragon escapes from its cave and goes on a rampage, killing a Christian priest and generally wreaking havoc. A new lottery is held, and the princess removes all the names and replaces them with her own name, so she is chosen. The king, now desperate, gives Galen his amulet back and begs him to kill the dragon. The apprentice uses the amulet to enchant a heavy spear, while Valerian makes him a shield of dragon scales; as they prepare, the two realize they are falling in love.

Galen's rescue mission is delayed by an attack from Tyrian, whom the apprentice kills, but he is too late to prevent the princess from entering the dragon's lair. She is killed by Vermithrax's brood, young dragons who are in turn killed by Galen. He fails in his attempt to slay the mother dragon, though, and breaks his spear, escaping from the lair past a lake of fire.

Finally, Galen realizes his master's last wish. He returns to the lair and scatters the wizard's ashes over the lake of fire, and the old sorcerer regenerates. With only a limited time to live, the elder wizard allows the dragon to capture him and fly away. Galen understands that he must smash the amulet, which he does, and the wizard's body explodes, killing the great wyrm.

Galen and Valerian go off together, realizing that the time of wizards and dragons is coming to an end.

Dragonheart

Released in 1986, this movie is perhaps most noted for Sean Connery's role, providing the voice for Draco, the central dragon of the film. The serpent was originally going to be created from a model, but that idea was scrapped in favor of computer-generated images.

The hero is a knight, Bowen, who serves Prince Einon. When the prince is wounded and almost dies, he is saved by a dragon, who gives Einon a piece of his own heart with the promise that the prince will rule fairly and justly. However, Einon quickly turns into a cruel and brutal king. Bowen, believing that the dragon's heart corrupted the young man, swears vengeance against the serpent race and becomes a dragonslayer.

He's good at his job and eventually tracks down the last remaining dragon in the world, Draco. However, when Draco points out that if he dies, Bowen will no longer have a job, the two form a truce and, quickly, a partnership. They work a con game on the poor villagers of England: Draco arrives at a village and appears as if he will destroy it. The panicked citizens then hire Bowen to drive off or slay the dragon.

In the meantime, King Einon attempts to have his way with a peasant girl, Kara. She escapes and ends up seeking shelter with Bowen and Draco. Kara tries to start a rebellion against the corrupt ruler, but Bowen, a very capable fighter, refuses to help. Draco takes them both to Avalon, where they see the tombs of the Knights of the Round Table and are visited by the ghost of King Arthur. Bowen sees that he must do the right thing, and, with Draco, joins the rebellion.

We learn that Draco was the dragon who gave a part of his heart to the prince. Draco did this in the hopes of creating a lasting bond between dragons and men. The prince-turned-king and the dragon are linked by the heart, and so long as one of them lives, the other cannot be killed. Left with no choice, Bowen slays the dragon he has come to love, which results in Einon's death as well. The dragon's soul soars into the heavens to become part of the constellation for which he is named, and Bowen and Kara become the good and just rulers that the kingdom deserves.

Reign of Fire

Made in 2002, this film is set in a postapocalyptic near future, after civilization has been destroyed by an influx of dragons. As befitting its setting, it is a dark tale with very terrifying dragons as the enemies of man.

Workers excavating deep under London discover and awaken a huge dragon, which emerges to wreak terrible havoc; only one human, a boy named Quinn, survives this initial attack. A montage of newspaper clippings and news reports reveal that dragons then emerged from hiding all over the world. Humanity resists with our full arsenal of weaponry, but the resulting devastation only hastens the fall of civilization. Within a few years, dragons reign supreme over the world, and humans survive in isolated pockets. Survivors believe that the dragons last appeared millions of years earlier and exterminated the dinosaurs, then went into hibernation until the planet repopulated itself enough to support their return.

Ten years later, Quinn is the leader of a group living in a castle in Northumberland. His people are attacked by a dragon as they attempt to harvest a crop. All Quinn can do is drive the dragon away. Some time later, a group of paramilitary Americans, the Kentucky Irregulars, arrive. Their equipment includes a tank and a helicopter, and their leader is Denton Van Zan, who has devised a means of tracking and fighting dragons. Quinn is skeptical, but the two combine forces and kill the dragon that has been raiding the castle's farms.

Van Zan reveals his true plan: He believes that all the dragons around the world are females, and that there is one male, in London, that keeps regenerating the race. He knows that the females only live for a few months. If the patriarch dragon can be killed, he believes, the dragons' reign will end. Quinn refuses to help, fearing that the male is too lethal to be attacked, and he doesn't want to attract its attention. Van Zan goes anyway, drafting some of Quinn's men to help. The Irregulars are attacked before they can enter London, however, and most of them are killed.

Quinn's fears prove well grounded as the dragon does in fact trace the expedition back to the castle, which he attacks brutally. Van Zan returns, and together he and Quinn vow to go to London to kill the monster. They prepare explosive crossbow bolts to fire down the dragon's throat. They find the city crawling with dragons, with the male killing and eating many of the smaller wyrms. In the final battle Van Zan is killed, but Quinn finally has a chance to make the killing shot, and the dragon is destroyed.

After a few months, the last of the dragons have died out. Quinn's group establishes radio contact with a group of survivors in France, and the humans look forward to a long, slow time of rebuilding—*almost* certain that the dragons are gone for good.

Dragons on Television

Movies made for release directly to television generally lack the massive budgets and technical resources available to theatrical productions. However, because of the sophistication of modern computer-generated images, these films still offer an abundance of very "realistic" dragons.

George and the Dragon

This film was made for the Syfy channel in 2004, and as the title suggests a dragon is central to the plot. A huge female dragon is viewed as a terrible menace by the people of medieval England, and when the dragon kidnaps a princess this seems to prove the dragon's wicked nature. The captive princess witnesses the dragon lay a single egg, then (apparently) die.

Because she is a good-hearted woman, the princess determines to protect the egg through various adventures, thwarting the efforts of George—a knight just returned from the Crusades—who wants to destroy the egg. He becomes the protector of the princess, who is attempting to evade an arranged marriage to an ambitious prince. Naturally, the egg hatches and the mother dragon, not dead after all, returns to claim her offspring, interrupting a battle between George and the prince.

In the end, the dragon is revealed to be sympathetic to the main characters, as George spares her life. In return, the beast gulps down the evil prince who is just about to drive a sword through the hero's heart.

Wyvern

Produced as a combined Canadian and American venture in 2009, this film was originally shown on the Syfy channel. It follows many conventions of the classic monster movie, with an impressive computer-generated imagery (CGI) monster playing the title role.

The story is set in Beaver Mills, a small town in northern Alaska, at the time of the summer solstice and the midnight sun. Jake, an itinerant handyman/truck driver, and Clair, who runs the town's small café, together with the other townsfolk, are increasingly frightened by a series of disappearances and a violent, bloody attack against an isolated farm. One man, a retired colonel, has seen a flying serpent, but no one believes him.

The wyvern is in fact a two-legged dragon that has hatched because the ice containing its egg has thawed. The movie's unique version of wyvern mythology places them into the old tales of the Norse and includes a story of its creation as the offspring of one goddess, imprisoned in the ice by Odin himself.

During the solstice festival the wyvern attacks the town, killing many— including the sheriff and his lone deputy. It knocks down the radio tower and attacks and kills anyone attempting to leave the town by road. The characters are isolated, and the wyvern is clever enough to use a wounded man as bait to draw the others into range of an attack.

Eventually Jake, Claire, and the colonel discover a nest and several eggs in the woods. They load the eggs onto a truck, and Jake drives crazily along a mountain road with the wyvern in pursuit, drawn by its eggs. The monster latches onto the truck as Jake tumbles out the door, sending truck, wyvern, and eggs over a cliff to land in a blazing pyre.

CHAPTER 10

NOTABLE
DRAGONS
of Games

he first role-playing adventure game was *Dungeons & Dragons* (*D&D*), which was created in the early 1970s. As the name suggests, these great, mythical serpents played an important role in many a *D&D* campaign. True to their mythology, dragons in *D&D* and other role-playing games can serve as adversaries or allies to the characters who are experiencing the adventure itself. In a significant departure from almost every other type of table game on the market, the players of a *D&D* game seek to work together, cooperating so that their characters can achieve a common goal.

In the years since *Dungeons & Dragons* was first introduced to the world, a host of other games have followed in its footsteps. At first, role-playing games were played with miniature figures, dice, and paper sheets of character statistics and game rules. As the decades passed, however, many of the gaming venues became computer driven. Further evolution of the hobby came with the introduction of massive multiplayer role-playing games, such as *World of Warcraft*, which allow several players to work as a team or as competitors as they try to overcome challenges and attain treasures and other objectives.

No matter how many incarnations this hobby experiences, however, the imprint of the original inspiration remains: A player takes on the role of a heroic character and battles threats and challenges . . . including dragons.

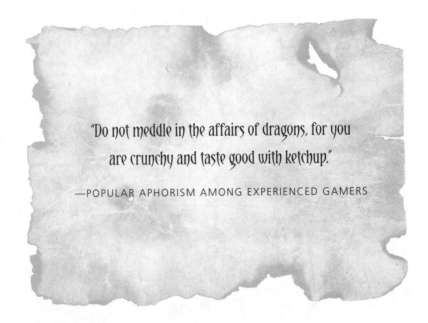

"Do not meddle in the affairs of dragons, for you are crunchy and taste good with ketchup."

—POPULAR APHORISM AMONG EXPERIENCED GAMERS

The Role of the Dragon in an RPG (Role-Playing Game)

In a traditional RPG, a dungeonmaster serves as a sort of storyteller/referee, describing the game environment to the players (each of whom is represented by a character) so that the players can make decisions and choose actions. The results of these actions, whether to attack, flee, negotiate, explore, or so forth, are adjudicated by the referee. In addition to determining the results of specific actions, the referee plays the roles of all of the characters and creatures that the players' characters encounter during the course of the adventure.

Because a role-playing campaign is bounded only by the imaginations of the referee and the players, an infinite set of possibilities avail themselves. A dragon in a game world can guard a treasure trove or hold an innocent captive hostage. Dragons can likewise appear in a helpful guise, offering counsel to the players or issuing commands and exhortations.

The Dragons of *Dungeons & Dragons*

In the original fantasy role-playing game, dragons were divided into two classes. Each class was readily identified by appearance, and each shared at least the bare bones of a similar moral code. Very generally speaking, dragons identified by their color (red, green, black, etc.) were evil creatures and typically served as adversaries to the players. Dragons identified by the metal their scales most closely resembled (copper, brass, silver, etc.) were more benign and more likely to serve as allies and helpmates to the players. This is not a hard and fast distinction, and clever characters may appeal to the better nature of even an evil dragon; and foolish characters have no difficulty in offending a good dragon.

Dragon Features

Whatever its color, size, nature, and temperament, a *D&D* dragon possesses the typical Western dragon form: a long, supple neck with a crocodilian head; jaws that can open wide and are lined with sharp, slightly curved fangs; four muscular legs, and taloned, powerful feet; a long and whiplike tail; and two broad, leathery wings. All dragons can fly.

Generally, the dungeonmaster decides on the exact quantities of these traits, depending on the abilities (or lack thereof) of the characters. However, the game includes rules allowing the referee to roll dice to randomly determine, for example, the age of a particular dragon.

A WINGLESS DRAGON?

One possible exception to the typical body description of a *D&D* dragon is the gold dragon, which is sometimes portrayed in a style more typical of a Chinese dragon—that is, an even longer body that lacks wings.

Dragon Ages

The age of a dragon can range from very young to ancient—the latter being dragons that are more than 400 years old. Naturally, a dragon's age has a great deal of influence on its strength, size, lethality, and cunning. This is reflected in the amount of damage it can inflict with its bite, crushing talons, and lethal breath.

Dragon Senses and Aura

Dragons are blessed with exceptional vision and, to a certain extent, can see even under pitch dark conditions. Their hearing is also very keen, and they possess a powerful sense of smell. Because of the aura of magic surrounding these mighty wyrms, dragons are even able to see creatures and objects that are protected by invisibility spells.

Dragons possess their own aura, which affects characters and other creatures, such as horses, in the presence of the wyrm. The effects of this aura can range from outright panic and flight to paralysis to limitations on a character's fighting abilities brought about by the realization that one is threatened by or is fighting such a formidable foe.

Dragon Speech

Dragons are generally at least equal to the average human in intelligence, and some of them are considerably smarter. All dragons can speak at least their own draconic tongue, and many of them know other languages. Many dragons are social, even gossipy, and enjoy conversational interaction—even if their eventual intention is to turn their conversational partner into an appetizer. Dragons are naturally curious and can often be lured into long, life-preserving conversations, merely because they want to find out everything the character knows or chooses to share.

Dragon Breath

All *D&D* dragons possess at least one type of breath weapon, often their most lethal form of attack. Fortunately for the survival of many characters, breath weapons can only be employed a limited number of times. While of course the fire-breathing dragon is a staple of Western dragon mythology, not all dragons breathe fire—the exact type of breath weapon a dragon possesses depends on what kind of dragon it is.

Whatever the breath weapon, its effects are determined in some part by the dragon's size and age. Naturally, the larger the dragon, the more potent will be its breath.

Dragons and Magic

As if a lethal breath weapon and a powerful bite are not threat enough, many dragons can cast magical spells. Again, the chances of a dragon possessing this ability are based on the intelligence and age of the dragon. Because dragons are lethal enough in their physical form, dragon spells are often used to conceal themselves or to confuse, or otherwise trick those who have had the misfortune to encounter the great wyrms. Spells that help to protect a treasure trove are of particular use to dragons. Regardless of type, dragons in *D&D* are always jealous and possessive of their valuables.

Evil Dragons

The dragons that generally serve as villains and monsters in *Dungeons & Dragons* are known as the chromatic dragons. Characters who encounter a chromatic dragon—and who have done their homework!—will at least know what type of breath weapon and what level of intelligence they are likely to face.

Chromatic dragons have probably collected masses of treasures over their lives, and typically guard those treasures viciously. Some dragons collect tribute from the local population, including sacrificial captives, and keep those offerings—or the offerings' remains—as parts of their collection.

Evil dragons tend to be very territorial, even in the presence of their own kith and kin. Many older evil dragons bear the scars of duels with other dragons, and a small chromatic dragon who encounters a large one of another species will almost certainly flee to avoid being killed. Chromatic dragons will eat dragon flesh—though usually not from a dragon of the same color as the killer itself.

Black Dragons

Black dragons are among the more stupid and venal of the great serpents, probably the closest in resemblance to the actual snakes of the wild that are their ever so distant cousins. These dragons dwell in damp and dark places, preferring swamps that are well shaded with jungle foliage, or deep caves that are reasonably warm and well supplied with water. They disdain sunlight, though the rays of the sun do not do them any particular harm; and they much prefer warm environments to cold. A full-size black dragon can attain a length of perhaps as much as thirty feet.

In battle, a black dragon prefers to attack from ambush, even against a weaker or unarmed foe. They are capable, like alligators and crocodiles, of almost completely submerging in water so that only their eyes and nostrils are exposed. They are good swimmers, and prefer to fight in the water or on the ground rather than in the air.

The breath weapon of a black dragon is a stream of lethal and corrosive acid that spews forth from the creature's mouth out to a range of about sixty feet.

Blue Dragons

Blue dragons dwell in deserts and other dry regions, disdaining the presence of water. Shrewd and cunning, a blue dragon will seek to amass as much treasure as it can. They prefer caves but quite willingly will occupy an old ruin or other abandoned habitation. (In fact, blue dragons have been known to provide powerful incentive for previous occupants to abandon said habitations!) They are also capable of and willing to excavate deep pits in sand and will also work diligently to carve sandstone formations into lairs or fortresses.

As a result of their superior intelligence, blue dragons can use negotiation, threats, and intimidation to further their ends—which, barring other considerations, generally revolve around gaining more treasure for their hoard.

A blue dragon spits a destructive lightning bolt as its breath weapons. These bolts can strike targets as far as 100 feet away. Blue dragons are larger than blacks, and a full grown blue might be as long as forty feet or more from nose to tail. They can conceal themselves in sand, but are generally arrogant and confident enough that they do not feel the need to attack from ambush or to hide from any potential threat.

Green Dragons

If black dragons are the closest in appearance to their draconic cousin, the snake, green dragons are most closely evocative of another relative, the lizard. These wyrms are often distinguished by a jagged fin running down the spine and the full length of the neck as far back as the shoulders of the monster's forelegs. Green dragons, like most of their kin, seek caves or other underground locations to make their lairs, but they will often dwell in the midst of a forested wilderness. Often, the trees and other plants in the vicinity of a green dragon lair will have an unhealthy look, as they tend to suffer from the noxious vapors associated with the wyrm's breath.

Greens are among the most aggressive and confrontational of all the great wyrms. Often they will attack without warning and without any obvious reason to do so. They are not very picky eaters, consuming almost anything that they can find in their forested domains, but they value the flesh of elves and will actively hunt the members of that exalted race.

Green dragons that can talk are most definitely not to be trusted. They pride themselves on deceit and are ill tempered and greedy. These emerald serpents are only of average intelligence, however, and can sometimes be defeated through cleverness and trickery. The breath weapon of a green dragon is a lethal cloud of poisonous gas; naturally, the dragon is immune to the effects of its own poison. Green dragons are mid-sized by comparison to their kin, with the largest attaining a length of perhaps thirty-six feet.

Red Dragons

Red dragons are the largest, fiercest, and probably the most evil of all the chromatic dragons. They are terrible enemies and will easily carry a grudge for more than a human's lifetime. When truly aroused, a red dragon will attack its foe's family, lands, and even descendants.

A huge, ancient red dragon can attain a length of nearly fifty feet. They tend to make their lairs in rugged terrain, such as rocky hills or craggy mountains, though they disdain the freezing temperatures of the loftiest heights. Like other dragons, they prefer to dwell underground.

The breath weapon of a red dragon is a cloud of billowing flame. The largest dragons can spew this flame out to a range approaching ninety feet. Because of their extreme cruelty, however, red wyrms often prefer to dismember their prey more slowly by using their powerful foreclaws.

White Dragons

Sometimes known as "frost dragons," the whites are denizens of icy wastes, often dwelling among the very highest mountains or in the polar reaches of glacier and snow. Whites are probably the least intelligent of all the chromatic dragons, tending to be even less clever than the blacks. The majority of them have never learned to speak a human language, and magic use among white dragons is exceptionally rare. Perhaps because they survive in such hostile environments, they seek to avoid interaction with other dragons.

The breath weapon of a white dragon is a blast of lethal frost expelled in an expanding cloud. That blast can freeze exposed flesh instantly and may

leave a lingering fog in the air that will help to conceal the dragon's next move—whether it is to continue a battle or beat a hasty retreat.

White dragons tend to be the smallest of the chromatic wyrms, and it is extremely rare for one to reach a length of greater than twenty-five feet.

Good Dragons

Dragons with scales the hues of various metals are referred to as metallic dragons. They are not as bloodthirsty or instinctively violent as the chromatic dragons, but they don't make cuddly pets, either. Like all of the great serpents, metallic dragons are vain and proud, frequently avaricious, and take great delight in their triumphs. They view humans, dwarves, and other races as inferior, and they are rarely motivated to help players' characters out of the goodness of their hearts. Stealing a treasured possession from the hoard of a silver dragon is every bit as foolhardy and dangerous as stealing from a red.

A metallic dragon may be persuaded to help in a worthy cause, possibly to defer fatal punishment of a transgressor or to perform a useful service. But the dragon must have a reason that makes sense to it.

Metallic dragons sometimes collect treasure with a selective eye. Paintings, tapestries, carvings, and so forth might appeal to the artistic senses of a refined silver dragon, for example.

Brass Dragons

The brass dragon is one of the most social of the great wyrms. Many speak languages known to humans, and they will spend hours in conversation. They can be friendly to those who show them proper respect. Brass dragons are imaginative, and their ideas about protocol may be difficult for a visitor to understand. They also enjoy tricks and pranks, and for this reason are said to have a wicked sense of humor.

The brass dragon prefers arid surroundings and warm temperatures. They make their lairs underground but avoid tight quarters. If no suitable subterranean space is available, a brass dragon may dwell in some desert gorge or canyon with precipitous walls.

Brass dragons are medium-size, with the largest reaching a length of perhaps thirty feet. Unlike chromatic dragons (and some other metallics) brass dragons do not have a lethal breath weapon. Instead, they breathe a cloud of gas that can either induce sleep or inspire terror in those who breathe it.

Bronze Dragons

These metallic serpents enjoy water and will often make their lairs near large lakes or seas. Islands with natural caves are a favorite habitat of bronze dragons. They have a strong sense of justice, and unlike brass or copper dragons, may sometimes be persuaded to undertake a course of action to right a great wrong. They can reach a pretty good size, with the longest extending around forty feet from nose to tail.

Bronze dragons are exceptionally curious and are especially interested in the behavior of humans. These wyrms have the unique ability to shift shape into the form of some animal and will often disguise themselves thus in order to observe and study humans. Every bronze dragon has at least one animal shape that it can take, while the cleverest can assume any of several different forms.

Bronze dragons, like brass, have a selection of two different breath weapons. One is a lightning bolt very similar to the breath of a blue dragon. The other is a cloud of noxious gas that generally repels intruders and other undesirables.

Copper Dragons

Copper dragons are the merry pranksters of the serpent world. They love trickery and surprises, enjoy mockery, and are masters of sarcasm. Even in battle, they will attempt to taunt and goad their opponents into making rash attacks. However, they are notoriously thin-skinned and sensitive when it comes to their own pride and are very quick to take offense at any attempt to poke fun at the dragon itself. They appreciate a good story, however, and can often be distracted by a character who can weave such a yarn, especially one that is funny or reveals a self-deprecating side of the storyteller.

The body of a copper dragon is supple and powerful, and they can move with a catlike grace. They can pounce great distances and often use their prodigious leaping ability in combat. They can scale walls, cliffs, and other vertical surfaces with ease and often seem to prefer climbing to flying.

Perhaps as a result of this spider-like ability, copper dragons like to make their lairs in narrow places with very high roofs overhead. They will scuttle up and down the walls in spaces too compact to allow a dragon to spread its wings.

Copper dragons are medium to large size, attaining a maximum length of some thirty-six feet at full maturity. Like the other metallic wyrms, they can use either of two breath weapons: a blast of caustic acid or a cloud of gas that causes anyone who breathes it to become sluggish, clumsy, and slow.

Gold Dragons

Gold dragons are perhaps the most benign and admirable wyrms of the entire serpent world. They despise bullies and have a very low tolerance for injustice. They are reflective and contemplative, and cherish beauty and harmony. They are the only dragons that, sometimes, do not have wings. Whether winged or not, a gold dragon's scales resemble that same metal. Their long bodies are smooth and supple, and they can move with exceptional grace. They are among the largest of all dragons, and full-grown specimens have been known to exceed fifty feet in length.

Gold dragons can change their shape into that of any other animal, no matter what its size. These great serpents frequently use this ability to observe the life of the world without having to create the side effects that their awesome selves invariably produce. A gold dragon can comfortably shape shift for years, even decades, at a time, and they have been known to wander the world as sages, hermits, and other apparently feeble, elderly humans.

For their lairs, gold dragons are not particularly concerned with the surrounding environment, be it mountain, forest, swamp, savannah, or shore. They are comfortable dwelling in cities and towns, though in this case they will do so in the form of a human, elf, or other person. However, they do prefer their dwellings to be made of stone, rather than wood or brick.

Although they tend to be patient and even-tempered, when aroused, a gold dragon is a terrifying and mighty foe. In its true draconic form, it is a massively powerful creature and will not hesitate to employ magic.

Gold dragons can employ one of two different breath weapons: a blast of fire or a gas that induces fatigue or weakness in those who inhale it.

Silver Dragons

Silver dragons are among the most beautiful of creatures, regal and majestic when fully grown, shimmering like liquid metal with an almost mirror-like brightness. Of all dragonkind, they seem to have the most kinship with humans, and a silver dragon can take the form of a man or woman (of the same gender as the dragon) for extended periods of time. Like gold dragons, they often change their shape so that they can observe the activities of humans. Unlike the golds, however, who often tend to remain aloof to human affairs, the silvers willingly join in those endeavors under the guise of their two-legged identities.

For their lairs, silver dragons seek high places. They love high mountains, and will seek to find caves there. They will expand the cracks and gaps caused by frost and erosion, shaping the places into suitable caves. Silver dragons also have a unique ability to walk, stand, and rest upon the clouds themselves. Some silvers are even said to have made their lairs in the clouds, though it seems likely that most prefer to have more solid surroundings for protecting their treasures and laying their eggs.

The two breath weapons of the silver dragon give it a choice of a lethal and a nonlethal attack. For its deadly exhalation the silver can blast forth a cloud of frost. Alternately, the silver dragon can breathe a cloud of paralyzing gas.

Unique Dragons

Two dragons named in the early *Dungeons & Dragons* books were established as the mistress of the chromatics and master of the metallics. These are beings of great cosmic import, closer to gods—or at least demigods—than to mortal creatures.

Tiamat

Named for the founding goddess of ancient Babylonian and Sumerian myth, this horrific creature is rarely encountered, but when she is her opponents assume she has emerged from some nether plane of existence—perhaps even one of the levels of Hell itself.

Her body is a massive—some sixty feet long—and corrupt image of the chromatic dragons, for she has five heads, each of a different color. Thus, all the chromatics are represented by this demonic embodiment of evil and power.

Tiamat hates all representations of virtue and beauty, and she will kill and destroy for the sheer joy of creating destruction. She is vain to an extravagant degree and may be briefly forestalled by flattery, but she has contempt for weakness and is quite likely to torture anyone who arouses her disdain. It is said that, on her own plane of existence, she has whole fortresses of dungeon cells, in which legions of her enemies have been imprisoned, kept (barely) alive only so that they can be tortured by the great monster or her corrupt and foul minions.

Tiamat never sleeps, and she is a powerful magic user. She can cast spells from each of her heads. She can travel via teleportation, though she can also fly. Her wings are powerful, but her sheer size and bulk makes it difficult for her to maneuver around obstacles or in the midst of aerial combat. Tiamat can also change shape into any living creature, but she is too vain to do this very often—she much prefers to present the horrific grandeur of her true form to anyone who encounters her.

She is reputed to guard a massive hoard of treasure, wealth beyond the scope of even the greediest adventurer's imagining. But as her lair remains virtually inaccessible, on some remote plane of existence, no one in living memory has seen those treasures—at least, no one who has returned to tell the tale.

Generally, Tiamat assigns her minions to do her fighting for her. She demands tribute from those she favors with her commands, and even the most selfish of lesser dragons know better than to try and cheat their mistress out of such rewards as she thinks are her due. If pressed, however, she is a formidable combatant, since each of her five heads can bite savagely or exhale the breath weapon consistent with that color of chromatic dragon.

Bahamut

Also known as the "Platinum Dragon," Bahamut is the king, or lord, of all the metallic dragons. Whereas Tiamat's lair is reputed to exist on some level of Hell, Bahamat lives in a great palace that shines in some celestial domain—some say it lies "behind the east wind." Bahamut is much more likely than his villainous counterpart to be encountered in the mortal world, however, since he delights in traveling among humans, usually in the guise of some elderly sage. He has the power of teleportation and can change his shape into any living creature he chooses.

Bahamut places great stock in human virtues, including generosity, kindness, and mercy. He admires those who serve as champions for the weak and has been known to reward those who particularly impress him with worthy deeds.

Bahamut has a group of companions who serve as his guardians, disciples, and acolytes. They number seven and will often appear as meek and innocent beings, such as children, monks, or even as dogs or canaries. These seven consorts are in fact powerful gold dragons; like their master, they delight in a friendly and harmless appearance—at least, until someone comes along and tries to bully the old man and his seven pet birdies, for example.

In his dragon form, Bahamut is more than seventy feet long, with a slender body and gossamer wings that are almost transparent. If roused to battle, he can choose one of three different breath weapons: a blast of lethal frost; a cloud of gas that causes the targets to become gaseous and insubstantial themselves; or a blast of sound that can shiver castles, even great cliffs, into pieces.

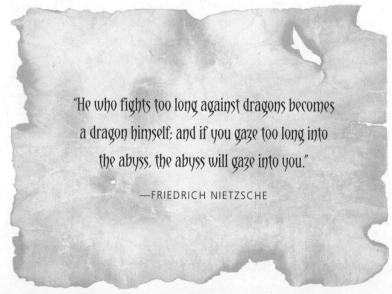

"He who fights too long against dragons becomes a dragon himself; and if you gaze too long into the abyss, the abyss will gaze into you."

—FRIEDRICH NIETZSCHE

Notable Dragons of Other Role-playing Games

Because they are central to so many interpretations of heroic fantasy, dragons play an important part in the universes of many fantasy role-playing games. In some of these games dragons are numerous, while others contain just a few mighty serpents. Many high-quality and popular games feature dragons, and while it's not possible to list them all, here are some of the most interesting.

Stormbringer

First published in the early 1980s by Chaosium, and featuring Michael Moorcock's character Elric of Melnibone, the *Stormbringer* game includes several notable dragons. In fact, it was later published with an updated game system under the title *Dragon Lords of Melnibone.* The inspiration for the games in all their editions remains the epic stories written by Moorcock.

The dragons of Melnibone are an ancient, powerful race, symbols of the royal throne. These are not fire-breathing dragons—instead, they exhale a venomous and flammable gas. It was said in the ancient days that a dragon must sleep for a full century for every day that it is active, and in that era there were a great number of dragons inhabiting the world and dwelling and resting in its deep, sunless caverns.

By the time the ancient empire began to fade from its vast breadth to a single surviving city, the number of dragons was drastically reduced. When they were summoned to the ultimate battle by Elric's mighty horn, less than 100 of them appeared to serve him. In times past their numbers would have darkened the skies.

Pendragon

Inspired by and set during the time of King Arthur, *Pendragon* is a fantasy game, first published by Chaosium, later produced by Green Knight

Publishing, and finally rereleased by White Wolf, Inc. The emphasis of the game is on human quests and the creation of heirs and dynasties. However, dragons and other magical creatures are present in the game. The dragons, in particular, are so dangerous to characters who encounter them that they are best left unmolested by players who wish to keep their characters alive—barring some terribly compelling reason to seek out and likely do battle with one of the great serpents.

ARTHURIAN DRAGONS

Curiously, the tales of King Arthur and the Knights of the Round Table contain very few accounts involving dragons. The knights often encounter other knights or strange and supernatural guardians and monsters—but very few dragons. When dragons do appear, though, they are very important. The magician Merlin, at one point, prophecies that a certain tower built by the ruler Vortigern cannot stand because two dragons, one red and one white, struggle eternally beneath its foundations. Both Lancelot and Tristan, the greatest knights of Arthur's court, encounter and kill dragons.

Chivalry & Sorcery

Published in 1977 by Fantasy Games Unlimited, *Chivalry & Sorcery* was one of the first competitors to *Dungeons & Dragons* to be professionally produced and marketed. With a greater emphasis on "realism" than *D&D*, *Chivalry & Sorcery* still allowed players to take the role of heroic characters, though there was more emphasis on actual historical inspiration for the settings, especially regarding feudalism and the church. The game has undergone several revisions and new editions through the years. It contained two significant dragons, which were uniquely detailed examples of mighty serpents.

The Blatant Beast

This unusual creature is a powerful dragon, well capable of slaying and devouring even skilled and competent adventurers. The Beast is very sensitive to its status, and insists upon being treated with the utmost respect—for instance, in conversation it must be referred to as "My Lord" or "Your Grace."

The most remarkable aspect of the Blatant Beast, however, is its fondness for poetry. It will often offer its intended victims a chance to avoid a horrific fate if they can recite an amusing or moving bit of verse. Characters such as bards have a better chance of saving themselves, though anyone can take a stab at it. If the dragon enjoys the poem, he will let the poet and his companions live—and if he is greatly impressed, the dragon might even offer some useful information or other assistance to the wandering adventurers.

The Questing Beast

Most people don't believe this monster is a dragon, but it is so hard to find, that its true nature is difficult to discern. It is possible that no one has ever seen the Questing Beast in its true form. It has a couple known abilities, however: It can change shape into the form of many different forest animals, and it can cast a spell upon certain bold adventurers, sending them off on a quest that is unlikely to end successfully. These are certainly similar to a dragon's abilities.

DragonRaid

First released in 1984, this game is unique in that it is an evangelical Christian role-playing game, designed to teach players many lessons gleaned from the Bible. "Spells" cast by the player are, in many cases, literal verses from the books of the Bible.

Not surprisingly, the dragons in this game all serve the forces of evil, and the heroic characters, questing in the name of Jesus, seek them out in the Dragon Lands. The serpents themselves represent the most potent forces of Satanic power and are, essentially, demons.

Bushido

This game, originally published in 1979 by Tyr Games (later, Phoenix Games, then Fantasy Games Unlimited), is the first popular game to use an Asian setting. Characters play the roles of warriors, ninjas, monks, and so forth. Despite its complicated rules, it has been a popular game and features many dragons drawn from Asian settings, most notably Japan. The dragons can function as adversaries or allies to the players, and they tend to be immensely powerful.

Shadowrun

This science-fantasy game published by FASA Corporation in 1989 is set in a near-future world that mingles elements of technology and magic. Much of the game action occurs in Seattle, Washington, although Denver,

Colorado, and New York City are also featured. Because of a cosmic shift in the ages of the world, beings such as dwarves, elves, and trolls can be found in mid-twenty-first century America.

Among these exotic creatures are dragons that, in *Shadowrun*, tend to have personalities, intelligence, and values not unlike humans. Dragons in this game world are organized, and even employ subordinates working in networks to support, protect, and otherwise help them. Many of these dragons can also change shape and are known to frequently employ human forms.

The game materials describe several notable dragons, including Dunkelzahn and Alamais.

Dunkelzahn

This mighty dragon is said to have awakened in a Colorado lake during 2012, the time dragons began to appear all over the world. Dunkelzahn was immediately interviewed by an ambitious newswoman, and as a result he became a celebrity and, soon, the host of his own television show, *Wyrm Talk*. His fame and reputation was such that he was eventually granted U.S. citizenship and was even elected President of the United States during the 2050s—a term that lasted less than a single day, due to his assassination while he was in human form near the Watergate Hotel in Washington, D.C.

Alamais

Like Dunkelzahn (with whom he would exchange a fruitcake every Christmas season) Alamais was a Great Western Dragon who had slumbered for thousands of years before the awakening of 2012. He mostly resides in Germany and is politically active. In addition, he controls several large corporations. He is large and very powerful and once survived a direct hit scored upon him by an orbital laser.

Iron Kingdoms

This role-playing game, published in 2004 by Privateer Press, adds steam power, firearms, and some early uses of electricity to the typical fantasy environment. There are very few dragons in the world, but those that exist are ancient, powerful, virtually immortal, and irredeemably evil. They possess a life force, called *athanc*, which persists even if the dragon's physical body is somehow destroyed. From the athanc, the creature can cause itself to be reborn.

Dragons in this setting are so foul and vile that their mere presence causes plants to wither and die, or be corrupted by the serpent's powerful evil. That evil essence can also claim the souls of lesser creatures, making them the dragon's slaves. The blood of a dragon can be used to create a kind of offspring, dragon spawn, which can be forced to serve the creating dragon.

One *Iron Kingdoms* dragon, Lord Toruk, is considered by many characters in the game to be a god, and by many others to be a heretical imposter. He is the eldest and original dragon. At one point he tried creating lesser dragons as followers, but when they acted independently he hunted down as many of them as he could catch, devouring them and reincorporating their athanc back into himself.

Additional Games with Dragons

Some other RPGs that include dragons are *Earthdawn* (FASA, 1993), with its Cathay, or Asian, dragons, as well as the mighty Greater Dragons; *RuneQuest* (Chaosium, 1978), with its detailed, and dragon-rich, world of Glorantha; *Tunnels & Trolls* (Flying Buffalo, 1975); *Ars Magica* (White Wolf Games, 1987), with its medieval European setting—including dragons; and *Pathfinder* (Paizo Games, 2009), which is a recent edition that develops and expands on the original *D&D* rules.

Notable Dragon Presence in Video and Computer Games

Much of the emphasis of role-playing games in recent decades has moved from friends sitting around a table, rolling dice, to people sitting at computers and interacting with electronic images of games portrayed on their monitors. At first, this was a solitary endeavor—and remains so with a great many "shoot 'em up" games, some of which present dragons as potential adversaries.

One of the most effective of these is *Skyrim* (Bethesda Softworks, 2011), which places great emphasis on the "realistic" special effects involved in human/dragon interaction. The primary adversary in the adventure is Alduin, a dragon who is destined to destroy the world. Along the course of the quest, players can meet dragons that will help them and battle dragons that oppose them.

Recently, higher-speed Internet connections and the desire for human interaction have opened up amazing possibilities for role-playing on a computer while still gaming with other people. In some cases, such as the massively multiplayer online role-playing game (MMORPG), players can work as teams from different locations around the globe, sharing experiences that are displayed on their game screens. Several of these games offer notable interactions—not necessarily fatal!—with dragons.

The most popular MMORPG in the (real) world is *World of Warcraft*, or *WoW*. Produced by Blizzard Entertainment and introduced to the market in 2004, *WoW* has had as many as 10 million subscribers at once and allows for a wide variety of fantasy world interactions. Incorporating many traditional aspects of role-playing games, it naturally presents dragons as both allies and adversaries to the players. It is even possible for a player, under the right circumstances, to gain a dragon mount for his or her character!

"Hope that you may understand!

What can books of men that wive

In a dragon-guarded land,

Paintings of the dolphin-drawn

Sea-nymphs in their pearly waggons

Do, but awake a hope to live

That had gone

With the dragons?"

—W. B. YEATS, "THE REALISTS," 1916

Index

About the Author

DOUG NILES has written more than forty novels and an extensive assortment of nonfiction books and articles. He is best known as an author of adventure fantasy, but also writes frequently in the military history and science fiction arenas. He has written many novels and short stories for the shared worlds of TSR, Inc. (now Wizards of the Coast), including the Dragonlance and Forgotten Realms series. Niles has also designed dozens of board and role-playing games. He is a former teacher who left that profession only because he had a chance to make a living while playing at his twin hobbies of writing and gaming. A confirmed Cheesehead, he lives in the countryside of Wisconsin with his wife (his two children having grown up and moved out) and two large dogs.